Little
Beach Book

Featuring

Judy Astley • Charlotte Bingham • Claudia Carroll

Kathy Lette • Anita Notaro • Jo Rees

Carmen Reid • Susan Sallis • Patricia Scanlan

Dear Reader

Whether you're reading this on a beach, in the back garden, in bed or the bathtub – welcome to a little you-time. The wonderful thing about a great book is that you can lose yourself in it anywhere – if the story's good enough even a hot and crowded bus won't spoil your pleasure. No wonder women love reading so much. In a hectic, busy and demanding world, we can just pick up a book and leave all our stresses behind.

In a recent survey of *Prima* readers 97% of you said that you read to unwind from the daily grind. (And a hilarious 63% confessed you'd much rather read in bed than get passionate with your partner! Sorry lads . . .)

So many of you enjoyed our exclusive collection of short stories last summer that we've put together another one for you by some of your favourite authors. And as an extra treat we've included some fabulous offers and competitions to really make your day. So dive in and enjoy!

Maire Fahey
EDITOR

TRANSWORLD PUBLISHERS
61–63 Uxbridge Road, London W5 5SA
A Random House Group Company
www.rbooks.co.uk

This sampler produced by Transworld Publishers
exclusively for *Prima* magazine and Virgin Holidays
Copyright © Transworld Publishers 2008

Addresses for Random House Group Ltd companies outside the UK
can be found at: www.randomhouse.co.uk
The Random House Group Ltd Reg. No. 954009

The Random House Group Limited supports The Forest Stewardship
Council (FSC), the leading international forest-certification
organization. All our titles that are printed on Greenpeace-approved
FSC-certified paper carry the FSC logo. Our paper procurement
policy can be found at www.rbooks.co.uk/environment

Typeset in 10/12pt Giovanni Book by
Falcon Oast Graphic Art Ltd.
Printed in the UK by CPI Cox & Wyman, Reading, RG1 8EX.

2 4 6 8 10 9 7 5 3 1

Contents

Smoke (and Fire)

JUDY ASTLEY

© Jon Astley

JUDY ASTLEY has been writing novels since 1990,
following several years as a dressmaker, illustrator,
painter and parent. She has two grown-up daughters
and lives happily with her husband in London and
Cornwall. The author of fourteen books published by
Black Swan, her new novel, *Other People's Husbands*,
will be published by Bantam Press in July. You can
find out more about her and her books on her
website: www.judyastley.com

'It's only a teenagers' barbecue. What can go wrong?'

Those nine words of 'wisdom' came from Flyn – Katie's father. They give you the gist of why we're divorced and why I'm so relieved that he now lives on the French side of the English Channel. His laid-back, 'hey, no worries' attitude to life that was so attractive when we were young and responsibility-free simply didn't work in the context of having to deal with grown-up life and raising a daughter. Too often I'd get home from work and find he hadn't bothered to take Katie to school that morning because 'Oh we fancied the zoo instead,' or 'Well, we were on our way, but there was this *fabulous* rainbow so we *had* to go and find the pot of gold.' Katie, of course, would be gleaming with delight at Flyn's anarchic naughtiness and, time and again, I'd be cast as Bad Cop for coming over all sensible and disapproving.

You couldn't say he wasn't a fun dad while he was on the premises though, I'll give him that. And full of surprises, oh yes. Once when I came home to a dark and empty house, I found a message on the answerphone to say he'd taken Katie out for lunch – in Paris. But bill-paying was a constant drama of court-action threats and his idea of deadlines (he's a freelance illustrator) had many an editor pulling their hair out. To live with, he was romantic, easy-going and creative but ultimately harder work than any number of small children. And then when he started being romantic, easy-going and creative with a red-haired woman he taught at his evening art group, it was time to call it a day.

So this is where we are now. I have the house and I work part-time sorting out tax muddles for people who are even flakier than my ex. Katie lives with me. Flyn has his half-built pile of old bricks among the lavender fields of Provence, his string of art-class floozies (French this time) and his painting. Katie goes to him for some of the holidays now that she's old enough to remind him when there needs to be more food in the fridge and she can work out what time to make him drive her to the airport in time for her flight home. Date-wise, men who light my personal touchpaper are few and far between – and I know it's boring and *sensible* but I wouldn't want Katie to see me notch up a string of failed relationships, so I'm not on the look-out for anyone.

Today is Katie's fourteenth birthday and Flyn called to wish her a happy day and to tell me that it's all going to be fine, which is easy for him to say from several hundred miles away. It's a glorious summer day, thank goodness, because how Katie is celebrating is what I unthinkingly agreed to back on a rainy April afternoon – a couple of dozen of her school mates over tonight for a barbecue in the garden. And I'm sure it *will* be just great. I persuade myself that fourteen is actually a lovely age – the sweet cusp of young adulthood, not necessarily the gateway to inevitable teenage hell; there's still a lot of the child in her and her friends, even though they all seem to have grown legs up to here overnight and their default stance involves a lot of pouting and hair-flicking (and that's just the boys . . .).

I'm graciously allowed to be present to cook the food (and only to cook the food – I'm to make myself scarce in some dark, remote corner of this house once I'm no longer of use) with the help of Siobhan, mother of Katie's friend Sara, so there won't be any playing-with-matches accidents and alcohol isn't on the menu. I've already had one father – of a sweet, quiet boy called Nick – on the phone, reminding me that if there are any drink-related incidents I will be held Personally Responsible – which is an odd term when you think about it. He really annoyed me there – does he think I've got no sense at all? That Siobhan and I would happily allow underage near-children to neck serious booze and risk them all being sick on my carpets or stomach-pumped in A&E? As if. Ridiculous. If I could frisk the guests for sneaked-in drink I'd have them lined up as they come in, like airport security.

It's at times like Katie's birthday and at Christmas that I miss the Flyn-and-me thing, because she's the one perfect item we created and shared and it would be lovely to have him here so we could agree that hey, with this, we did well. But if he *was* here I can imagine just what chaos it would be. Instead of using our barbecue, he'd be building a massive bonfire that would have our fence and next door's in flames in minutes. He'd have bought a couple of massively sensational celebratory fireworks that were way too hardcore for a suburban garden. Then Nick's dad would *really* have something to flap about. I sometimes think Katie finds me dull by comparison: sensible, staid. Well, all I can say is that living with Flyn, someone had to be the grown-up. Tonight I'll have the garden hose ready for accidental flare-ups. The first-aid box is on the kitchen worktop, primed against all teenage injury possibilities, including an extra box of tissues in case it's hearts that end up broken rather than bones. And please, I ask the gods, make it neither.

I've come across the Nick-father before, at a school parents' night a couple of months ago. He was bad-tempered then as well. I could tell because he and his wife were doing that thing where they call each other 'Darling' at the end of each sentence with a clenched-teeth spitty emphasis that tells you they're completely furious and close to hating each other. I'm a fairly curious person by nature but I wasn't going to hang around to overhear what the marital discord was about. I've had enough of all that at home in my time and besides, it was probably only about Nick's progress (or otherwise) in maths. Either way, that was then, but I sure as hell don't need bossy Nick Senior on my case today. He won't find anything to complain about – Siobhan and I have everything covered.

Except ... suddenly Siobhan *isn't* coming. Huge apologies, Sara tells me on the phone, but her mum's got flu and can't even get out of bed. Right. That's OK, really – no truly it is – the salads are ready in the fridge. The jacket potatoes are going to be cooked in the oven then finished on the flames. There's a birthday cake (because even though they all pretend to scorn such things, they'd be thoroughly miffed if there wasn't one) and Katie's favourite pud: chocolate mousse with straw-berries and those cat's tongue biscuits. Barbecuing is a simple enough skill and I can cook the Nigella-burgers and spicy chicken on my own easily enough. It's a bit late now to rope someone else in – I expect they've all made other Saturday night plans. And anyway, I suppose, really, what I'll miss is adult company – someone to talk to whose every sentence doesn't go up at the end, whether it's a question or not. Someone, come to think of it, whose every other word isn't punctuated with 'like'. Not that they'll talk to me, obviously, not beyond the strangely Midwich Cuckoo, over-smiley 'please' and 'thank you' with that sparkly eyed, so-innocent look that immediately makes you wonder what they're really up to.

Katie is in the garden with a couple of girls who've come early to help. They're hanging the twinkly fairy lights that we use at Christmas between the two apple trees. She's stuck garden flares along the pathway from the house and hung lanterns from the cherry tree. It's all going to look very pretty in the dark. I hope the neighbours think so when the music's blaring and twenty-four teenagers are shrieking and giggling and the boys have found a football – as boys always seem to – to kick at the fence. I'm watching her skipping about like a ten-year-old, but later she'll be in her tiny new flippy-skirted dress, so narrow that when she turns sideways she's the edge-width of a playing card. She'll be posing like a model with her eyes flickering back and forth to that moody, broody boy who looks like a junior rock star. Did I say this was a lovely age? A tricky, hellish, confusing one more like. Who'd be fourteen again? No one sane.

I'm in the kitchen assembling the kind of relishes they're going to want. There isn't enough tomato ketchup, I realize. Or that squirty American mustard they like. Kitchen paper too . . . It's no good, I'll have to go shopping.

'You OK out there, Katie?' I shout from the back door,

'I'm just going down to the supermarket . . . we still need a few things for tonight!'

A selection of 'Yeah/right/wha'ever' comes back at me, cheerfully enough. This is a good sign. All is well . . . so far.

There's something horribly depressing about late Saturday afternoon in a suburban supermarket. If you're living alone (or at least partnerless like me) it's just another of those places that emphasizes your singleness. As I eye up a lot of lone customers traipsing around with baskets of single-portion ready meals, I imagine that outside this chilly, half-empty shop is a smiley, happy world of jolly folks, all doing family activities. I picture parents in the park, taking photos as a child rides her bike without trainer wheels for the first time, or cheering a junior Wayne Rooney in the school football team. I have them all going swimming together or passing the popcorn along the row at the cinema. Mad, of course. If Dad is watching football it's probably on the sofa with a beer. Too many mums would be wasting their precious Saturday trailing a reluctant child to a shop for replacement school shoes which will be royally loathed.

The supermarket shelves are a messy mix of empty boxes and scattered goods. The regular staff are doing their best after the morning's busy blitz, which means the aisles are cluttered with bulky trolleys of stock to be unloaded. The weekend part-time kids can sense the end of their shift in sight and are sloping off behind the bread shelves to check in with their friends about the night's hot social possibilities via their mobiles. In my head, the list of things I need is growing. I'm going to need more than a basket so I return to the front of the store for a trolley. So far, I've picked up only the ketchup and, for myself for later, a bargain bottle of champagne in a fancy box, going cheap because its packaging says it's for Father's Day, which was a couple of weeks ago. Katie sent Flyn a card, rang him and got a sleepy female French voice on the end of the phone. I slope round the shelves rather gloomily, feeling bad about . . . well, feeling a bit bad on Katie's birthday. Trouble is, however much you're happy that your daughter is having a lovely day, it's one year older, one year nearer her leaving for good and then that'll be that. I can't help thinking as I look at Katie, who is now taller than me and keeps nicking my sable eye shadow, how short a time we get to keep our children. All that sighing and wailing new mothers do about lack of sleep with new babies, forever wishing for the next stage – I want to tell them to slow down, savour the moments. It's all gone in a blink and the next thing, your tiny baby is a big, independent near-adult checking her lipgloss in your rear-view mirror, agonizing over GCSE options and talking about university. I have a life, a job, brilliant friends, but Katie's been the main thing, and in a few speedy years I'll be waving her off and wondering if it's now the long, lonesome road to old age. Her attention will be on her own life, boyfriends, college, then career, home of her own some day, with luck. Will I have to resort to cats?

I need to cheer up. This is a rare and temporary mood-blip so I put too many medicinal bars of chocolate in the trolley and promise myself I'll have one glass of this champagne once the party-goers are safely off the premises . . . celebrate the success (oh please, fingers crossed) of Katie's party. The rest will keep. Till Flyn went, I never realized that those special champagne stoppers actually had a purpose.

'That's not for tonight, is it?' A voice breaks into my thinking as I fill a bag with tomatoes and contemplate the possibility of ratatouille with tomorrow's lamb.

'What?' I turn and look at the man who has spoken. He is pointing to my trolley, looking stern. Oh joy, it's him again, Nick's father. Does this man ever relax? He's got a trolley load of food and a twelve-pack of beers. Pot and kettle, but I don't comment. Instead, I say cheerily, 'The ketchup? Oh yes, it's for Katie's party. You can never have too much with teenagers. Your son's still coming tonight, isn't he?'

'Yes, he is. But I meant the champagne, not the ketchup. It's important that the adults in charge stay sober.' I frown and look at him, wondering if he's serious. Is he going to lecture me? He obviously really *does* think I've got no sense. Good grief, doesn't he realize he's talking to Mrs Safe?

'Look, Father-of-Nick,' I say it nice and slowly, just to make sure he gets the message. 'In spite of my being the kind of flighty divorcée who can't resist a cheap champagne bargain, I *do* know what's what. I've been a parent for as long as you have. I will *not* be drinking anything stronger than water tonight. I will be perfectly capable of driving an emergency injury to a hospital if it's necessary. And what's more . . .'

'Sorry!' he interrupts and smiles suddenly, and it's a good smile, one of those that crinkles his eyes at the edges into a little fan of lines. He must smile a lot because when he's not smiling, the lines are pale where the sun's tanned the rest of his skin. 'I'm just, you know,

16

a bit paranoid. It's my weekend to have Nick and I don't want any problems. You know how it is.' He shuffles about a bit, embarrassed that he's given something of himself away, I think. 'My ex-wife is forever nit-picking; she's sure I let Nick run wild while he's with me.'

'Well there's no chance of that on my premises, that I can promise. Everything's under control. Squeaky clean, that's me,' I tell him, a bit too sharply. But then, I have always been the Sensible One and I'm not having some stranger casually challenging that. I cross my fingers all the same, just in case the gods are planning a nasty, jokey surprise for me in terms of exploding chicken wings or minor lightning strikes.

We exchange a few more bits of party-conversation, (good weather for it, seems ten minutes since they were five – oh and he's called Mike) and off he goes, seemingly happy enough that I've reassured him. He's wished me a happy evening, says he'll see me later when he picks up Nick. He understands supermarket etiquette and tactfully takes off in a different direction from me. There's nothing worse than when you keep running into the person you've just been talking to as you trail each other round the aisles. What do you say? That inane 'We can't keep meeting like this' thing? No, exactly.

I collect all the items on my list and add enough food for several more days because I might as well while I'm here and go to pay for it all. Mike is two check-outs further along. He waves his fingers to me and gives me another of those creased-up smiles. The boy on my till is half-asleep. He keeps yawning and barely manages to move his hands, keeping his forearms resting on the edge of the conveyor. I half expect his drooping head to collapse on to my bag of potatoes, poor lad. He hardly looks at the goods and when they're all checked he grunts the total with absolutely no attempt at good customer relation skills. I resist the urge to ask for the magic word before handing over my debit card, because he hasn't said please. Time's running out now and this evening's going to be an exhausting one. By the end of it I'll probably find 'please' hard to come up with as well.

I'm just going out through the supermarket door, trying to remember whether the car is to the left or right of the car park, when an alarm goes off. I don't stop because I haven't got time now to indulge in the idle curiosity of seeing which poor sap has been caught with a stolen bag of carrots and my initial reaction when a security guard appears each side of me (and way too close) is to wish they would get out of my way because I'm running late. And then I look around and realize I'm the one who is being stared at. What's going on? What have I done? And why is Mike looking at me like that? What's so funny that has him helpless with laughter?

They've had a great time. The party couldn't have gone better. No one cut/burned/damaged themselves, no one had a tantrum because Boy A was talking too much to Girl B, no one gorged themselves on sneaked-in vodka and nobody discovered a dangerous latent allergy to spiced chicken. It's very late and Katie is now sitting out by the barbecue doing giggly post-party analysis with her two closest girl friends who are staying the night, oh and Nick of course. He's still here. That's because his father is here too. We're sprawled on the sofa with the champagne and the remains of the birthday cake, at last relaxing. It's been a long evening but we made a good team. He's a dab hand with a spatula and a burger and knows his way round a dishwasher, unlike most people who visit and cop out with, 'Oh I'll leave the loading to you . . . everyone has their special way of doing it, don't they?' The kitchen is immaculate, amazingly. I'd assumed Katie and I would tackle it in the morning but there's no need. Mike and I got it done, no problem.

'Thanks so much for tonight,' I tell him, raising my glass to him. 'I couldn't have done it without you.'

'Oh you could, Polly, you could,' he says then he laughs, 'but it would have been a bit of a rush. I mean, there are always little blips you can't factor into the best laid plans, aren't there? Even for someone as *sensible* as you. Someone so *squeaky clean*! Hah!'

'Yes well, I'd say most to-do lists for an event don't usually include "Get arrested for shoplifting". I think it comes under "unforeseen hiccups", don't you?'

'Don't know what you'd call it, but you made my day! "Everything's under control," you said! And so smugly! Love it!'

I laughed too . . . well you had to really. I should have been more on the ball, that's for sure. The half-asleep check-out boy simply hadn't put the bottle of champagne through the bar code thing. That was his fault. My fault was that I hadn't taken any notice of the total, hadn't taken in that it was light, by quite a few pounds. That'll teach me. As I handed over my receipt publicly to the security men I was outraged, certain that I, Mrs Sensible, couldn't possibly have failed to pay for something – well it was quite a shock. Once Mike had got over his hysterics at my comeuppance, he'd been sweetly helpful, coming with me to the manager's office, backing me up that I hadn't made any attempt to hide the bottle as I went round the store. I paid up and all was well. The worse that came out of it was that I lost valuable time and raced back to find Katie in a flap, saying everyone would be here 'like *really soon*?' . . . But there Mike was, first to arrive with his son and a promise to stay and help for the whole evening if I wanted. And yes, I found I did want, very much.

'So,' he says now, topping up my glass, 'what are you doing tomorrow? A spot of joy-riding? Working on getting that ASBO?'

'Ooh I hadn't thought!' I tell him. 'So many possibilities, so little time . . .'

'I suppose you wouldn't consider the sensible option then? You and Katie: lunch with me and Nick?'

'Hmm . . . it's between that and honing my breaking and entering skills. I'll have to think about it,' I tell him. But in truth, of course, I already have.

Mrs Plummer and the Golden Fish

Charlotte Bingham

© Carolyn Djanogly, *Image* magazine

CHARLOTTE BINGHAM comes from a literary family
– her father sold a story to H. G. Wells when he was
only seventeen – and Charlotte wrote her auto-
biography, *Coronet Among the Weeds*, at the age of
nineteen. Since then she has written comedy and
drama series, films and plays for both England and
America with her husband, the actor and playwright
Terence Brady. The author of many bestselling novels,
her latest novel, *The Enchanted*, will be published by
Bantam Books in August.

Binny was not aware that her neighbourhood was considered to be downtrodden, that it had been marked out for many years by estate agents as a *'not yet, but could be soon up and coming'* part of that great-hearted, boom, boom, boom, pulsating, I've-had-everything-thrown-at-me-but-I'm-still-here city known more generally to the rest of the world as London. Besides, although she lived in London, Binny, like most city dwellers, only really knew *her* bit of the city: her streets, her shops, her local friends.

Binny's parents were divorced, which in their case had led to a separation by countries, not just miles. Binny's father having been so unsuccessful because of his 'mucking about', as she called it, that her mother was understandably bitter.

Of course although she herself felt nothing but affection for where she lived, Binny was aware that her mother, Janice Dibden, felt that she had come down in the world, not just factually – she had been brought up in a much smarter part of London – but worse than that really, she had come down in the world in her *mind*.

There had been a time, she would remind Binny after two or four glasses of Chardonnay, when they had had a piano in the sitting room. There had been a time when there had been outings to the theatre and ballet, and friends in the country had asked them to stay for smart weekends. Now she could hardly afford a train ticket to Piccadilly, let alone to the Cotswolds.

Her mother had Binny's sympathy, she also had

Binny's brother's sympathy, so much so that he had joined the army at the earliest opportunity, not particularly because he wanted to be in the army, as he had explained to Binny, but solely because, with him out of the way, it would ease their mother's financial burden.

'Your mother is a very pretty woman, but her glass is not just half empty, it is completely empty. She needs to stroke the golden fish for luck,' their neighbour Mrs Plummer would tell Binny, looking over at the gold-coloured statue on the windowsill, before pouring Binny a cup of peppermint tea, and giving her a carefully sympathetic look. That look that told them both that Mrs Plummer understood her neighbour, and particularly her neighbour's mother.

At first, after they had moved to the new neighbourhood, the taste of Mrs Plummer's herbal tea had proved something of a stumbling block to their developing friendship. Much as Binny enjoyed the many comforts of Mrs Plummer's house – the velvet covered sofas, the paintings and the flowers – the taste of the tea did take a lot of getting used to, most especially since Binny had only been used to PG Tips, and Nescafé with condensed milk added (which, on cold mornings, before Binny left for her job at the insurance office, helped her get over her hunger pangs). Now, however, the tea, and the fire, and the gold in Mrs Plummer's huge earrings and necklaces, had all welded themselves inextricably into one.

The great thing about Mrs Plummer was that she was interested in Binny, so that made two of them. Binny and she were as one in their dreams of Binny being able to make her way in the world. It was an underlying thread in all their teatime conversations, in their

Saturday jaunts to the local market to buy vegetables, cheese and bread; and, of course, coffee, because next to teas with strange flavours, Mrs Plummer always asserted that she needed coffee as much as so many of the strange tropical plants in her conservatory needed rainwater.

Of course Mrs Plummer was always 'Mrs Plummer' to Binny, she would never have used her christian name. As a matter of fact Binny had no idea what it was. Besides, 'Mrs Plummer' sounded cosy, almost Christmassy, and it suited an older lady who still wore a hat and gloves to go shopping to the market, and who loved to cook.

'You can't teach someone to cook, Binny dear,' Mrs Plummer would say. 'You can *show* them how to cook, but you can't teach them to become a cook. Cooking is in here.' She would point to her heart. 'That is the place where it comes from, that is the true cook's real oven.'

Binny had long ago realized that her mother's oven was closed, and not only on Sundays, but for the whole week. It was not just because there were no men in the house for whom to care, it was because her mother had lost interest in anything that did not come out of a bottle. This was why when Mrs Plummer talked about her mother having a glass that was half full or half empty, Binny had to look away in an effort not to giggle. Her mother's glass was usually empty most of the time, because she had always drunk the contents.

The insurance office where Binny worked was bleak. There was no other word for it. It was not only her boss, Mr Dymchurch, a grey-suited man with a grey complexion, and a very dry manner that was always verging on sarcasm, it was everyone else in the building. Almost all favoured grey, and not just the men. Sometimes Binny would wonder what would happen if she went mad and turned up in scarlet or purple? Would everyone else turn the same colour? Of course, she never dared. She needed her job, and not just because she wanted to save up for a flat, which she had long ago calculated would come her way when she was just about to retire, but to help her mother, who was quite obviously unable to help herself, except to something in a bottle.

'Binny dear, your mother has a problem, you must face her with it.'

They were in Mrs Plummer's kitchen making a ragù bolognese to go with pancake cannelloni. Binny was so engrossed that she found she was quite unable to concentrate on anything else. The table was laid with a blue and white cloth, and Mrs Plummer was expecting two friends. One was a painter.

'He is from my youth, Binny dear, and mad as a hawk.'

When he arrived he looked far from mad. He was a handsome old man with a great head of thick white hair, and startlingly blue eyes.

'Just after the war I painted you in a Chinese red gown with a green dragon embroidered on one side. I sold it to a collector for a fortune, and in return, I just gave you the fish,' he reminisced to Mrs Plummer as he sat sipping red wine in front of the sitting room fire.

'You wanted me to drop the gown, Gregor, but I never would. I was not a professional model. Nor did

I want to sit about with goosebump skin, freezing in an arctic studio.'

'No, that was why I wanted to paint you. Now where is that nephew of mine?'

'He is on his way, I dare say.'

But he wasn't on his way at all. It seemed that Gregor's nephew had forgotten that he was meant to be coming to lunch, and had gone to Ireland in a private jet instead.

'He should have his ears boxed. Why did he not use his mobile phone which is always ringing when I take him to the theatre?' their guest growled, but Binny was more than relieved. The nephew sounded far too grand, and rich. She knew that Mrs Plummer had wanted her to meet him, but Binny knew that she would have little in common with someone who went about in private jets.

In the event they had a deliciously enjoyable Sunday lunch, with Binny having to contribute nothing in the way of conversation, and only too happy to serve up, and wash up, and do anything else that was necessary while she listened to stories from the fashion and art worlds of the 1940s, when the war had ended but there was nothing to eat and no fuel. Although judging from what was being said, everyone seemed to find delightful ways to keep warm without it.

'Dear Gregor, what a sweet man you are coming all the way from Chelsea to see me,' Mrs Plummer sighed, as her guest took his leave.

Binny held out his coat, a magnificent affair of many folds and pockets.

'May I?' He turned, still holding his hat, and pointed to the statue. 'May I, before I go?'

Mrs Plummer nodded and smiled as he went to stroke the golden fish.

'He gave me the golden fish for luck, and now he needs some back for himself.'

This gave Binny pause for thought. Perhaps if she could get her mother to stroke the golden fish as Mrs Plummer had once suggested, it would bring her luck too? It would not be easy. Her mother rarely left the house except to go to the hairdresser's salon on the corner, and then only on Monday afternoons when it was cheaper.

'Your poor mother will never come here,' Mrs Plummer told Binny in a firm voice. 'She knows how fond you are of me, how much time you spend here. That is enough to prevent her ever crossing the threshold.' She paused, giving Binny a considered look. 'I know how it is with this kind of woman, believe me. She is set like a blancmange in a mould, and no amount of shaking will loosen her out.'

Binny knew this to be true. She did not dare even mention the fish to her mother. Indeed the very thought of what her mother's reaction might entail was too frightening. The whole incident might well end up like something from a tabloid paper. A bitter woman was a frightening phenomenon. One mention of Binny's father and a look would come into Mrs Dibden's eyes that would have Binny shooting out of the front door and running wildly towards the office, or anywhere really, rather than stay at home. The look would reoccur if her father sent Binny a letter, or a present for her birthday, or even something cheerful like her mum's alimony money, which Binny imagined would have made most people happy. Not her mother.

*   *   *

It was a Saturday morning, which would usually occasion a trip to the market, but Mrs Plummer was away for the day. Lunch turned into tea. Binny's mother fell asleep, the day yawned on, then out of the growing dusk a dark green Bentley convertible drew up opposite Mrs Plummer's house. Binny, who was in the habit of keeping an eye on the place when her elderly friend was out, went at once to confront the owner of the car.

'Who are you?'

The owner of the Bentley stared down at the slim, dark-haired young woman in her jeans and white T-shirt.

'Who are you, please?'

She stared up at the tall, dark-haired man and his smart suit, gold watch and chic haircut.

'I'm here to see Mrs Plummer.'

'She's out for the day.'

'That's a pity. My uncle said just to turn up, she was always in—'

'You must be Gregor's nephew. You were going to come to lunch, but you went to Ireland instead.'

He seemed to sense her disapproval.

'Well, yes, I did.'

'What is it that you want?'

He pointed at the golden fish in the window.

'My uncle wanted me to look at it for her, it seemed she might want to sell it.'

It was difficult for Binny not to look appalled. The thought of Mrs Plummer having to sell her fish was too awful.

'It's not gold,' she said quickly, in case he was a very rich burglar. 'It's just Chinesey gold, nothing valuable.'

'Quite. Be kind enough to tell her I called, if you would.'

Binny watched him drive away, and then climbed on her bicycle. She would go for a ride in the park. It wasn't yet dark, the fresh air would do her good. She cycled fast, wondering all the time what it would be like to be that young man in his dark green Bentley. The words seemed to sing through her head. What would it be like, what would it be like? There was a strange sound, and at the same time the evening – Binny's evening – changed from dusk to dark in a matter of seconds.

Mrs Dibden stared at Mrs Plummer. She had never liked the woman, but now she *had* to like her. Mrs Plummer had driven her into the hospital every day for the past week. Despite the parking, the traffic jams, and the fact that Mrs Dibden sensed that she could ill afford the petrol, she had still climbed into her old Riley and driven Mrs Dibden into the hospital. She had even insisted on taking care of the parking, which was horrendously expensive.

'It's my pleasure, it's my pleasure,' she kept saying, which irritated Mrs Dibden, even though she knew it was irrational. How do you feel annoyed by someone so kind?

A week was a very long time to be driving a neighbour in and out of hospital. It was also a very long time to be unconscious, as Binny had been. The worst of it was, because Mrs Dibden always thought of herself first, that the wretched Plummer woman never insisted on going up to sit with Binny. She would merely murmur, 'No, no, thank you, you will wish to be alone with your daughter.' It was as if she sensed that Janice

Dibden would accuse her of trying to intrude, to take over Binny if she too went and sat by her bedside, and the niggling thing was that Janice knew that it was probably true.

'There is only one place for her to go with this sort of injury,' the consultant was saying. 'And that is—'

He named the hospital.

'But that is so far away from . . . from her home.'

Even as Janice said 'home' she felt embarrassed at her dishonesty. How could she call the house she had occupied with Binny 'home'?

'It will give her the best chance,' the consultant told her in a firm voice.

'Best chance,' Janice echoed, and reluctantly agreed.

So Binny, still unconscious, but clinging to life, was moved to the new facility where she had a room overlooking the garden, which she could not see, and modern paintings, and much that would have given her pleasure, had she been awake.

Here Mrs Plummer at last came to visit on her own, and she talked to her, firm in her belief that the unconscious can hear.

'I am leaving you the golden fish, Binny. Now you must wake up to stroke him, and he will bring you the luck you so badly need.'

Her mother was able to come on a cheap day return ticket, and seeing the golden fish beside her daughter's bed, she clucked her tongue.

'What is this doing here?' she asked one of the nurses, picking it up.

Before anyone could reply the miracle happened: Binny woke up. After which yet another miracle took place as her mother burst into tears, along with

31

all the nurses in the vicinity, although they could have no idea why Mrs Dibden crying was a miracle. How could they have known that she had not cried, or laughed, since her husband had run off with another woman.

'What exactly happened?' Binny asked Alexander, Gregor's nephew, only her second visitor since she'd woken to find her mother in tears, unable to make sense of it all. Binny was up and dressed but in a wheelchair.

'You were in an accident, just after we met outside Mrs Plummer's house. A car ran into you on your bicycle. You have been unconscious for days, until now.'

'What are you doing?'

'I am pushing you out into the garden,' Alexander told her.

He steered her chair under an old tree, and then sat down on a bench beside her. Binny started to laugh. He stared at her.

'You're like a Norland nanny with his charge,' she teased him. 'Mind you, male nannies are very fashionable these days.'

He smiled at her teasing, before a more sober expression crossed his face.

'I will be your nanny from now on, I will come every day now you are awake, help you with your therapy. Have you any memory of the accident?'

Binny would have liked to have shaken her head, but her neck was too stiff.

'I have been feeling so responsible, every day you were unconscious, I thought about you,' Alexander burst out.

She stared at him.

'You weren't involved?' Alexander was quite able to shake his head, lucky thing.

'No, no, well – yes.' As she stared at him, he continued. 'If I had not stopped and talked to you about the fish, those few minutes spent with me, well, it meant you had an accident. If I had just minded my own business, not gone to see the fish, you would have set off on your bicycle at a different moment. The idea haunts me. That time talking to me meant you had an accident.'

'Is that the reason you come to see me? Guilt? Because if that is the case, there is no need, truly there is not,' Binny told him, pride and hurt mingling in her voice.

Alexander looked at her, mortified, realizing his tactlessness.

'Good God no, I come to see you because I want to, truly I do.'

'You don't have to.'

He put out one elegant hand and laid it over Binny's.

'I know I don't have to, I have just told you, I want to.'

Binny looked away. 'Promise you won't feel sorry for me?'

'I promise, just so long as you promise to get better.'

Binny looked down. 'I will walk again, they said.'

'Medicine is wearing seven league boots, of course you will get better. I will make sure of it.'

Binny tried to smile. He leaned forward suddenly and kissed her briefly on the lips, and in that moment she believed him.

Of course neither Mrs Plummer nor her mother could visit her every day, the hospital was just too far away, so they knew next to nothing of Alexander's plans for Binny. He was plotting with the medical staff to have her flown to America for the latest treatments, treatments that would restore every part of her to her old self, but needless to say Alexander's Uncle Gregor spilled the beans.

'He is making plans, he is going to make her better in a trice,' he told Mrs Plummer.

'It will be very costly,' Mrs Plummer told Mrs Dibden with some satisfaction.

Nowadays they saw each other every day, crossing and re-crossing to each other's houses, and a miracle almost as magical as Binny waking from her coma happened to her mother. She swept and shone the house until it was as polished and gleaming as the golden fish. Out of gratitude to Mrs Plummer, Mrs Dibden cooked for her, and Mrs Plummer discovered that not only was Binny's mum a pretty woman when she smiled, but she was a most accomplished cook.

'I stopped, you know, when he ran off with my best friend.'

'Ah, a twin blow. That is harsh. But it happens, all too often.'

'Yes, on the other hand –' Janice Dibden gave Mrs Plummer a wry look, '– some might say, it was a twin relief. Perhaps they deserve each other. At the moment I hear they are very unhappy in Spain.'

'My dear.' Mrs Plummer smiled. 'Let us never mention them again. I have a theory that unhappy words beget unhappy thoughts, and only misery results. This crespoline is out of this world, and this wine, ah me! You have made a marriage in heaven.'

They stared at each other mischievously over the top of their wine glasses and clinked them, each thinking that perhaps the crespoline and the red wine were not the only heavenly marriage that would be made that year?

Of course they were right, as older ladies so often are, most especially when it comes to matches brought about by the gods, or in this case, by one small golden fish.

For, as Mrs Plummer stated with some satisfaction the following year when they were both choosing hats for the wedding of Binny Dibden to Alexander Smith-Brown, 'if I had not been low at the bank, and if Gregor had not come to lunch, and if he had not sensed that I was running out of funds, he would not have sent Alexander to see my golden fish. Binny would not have had an accident, Alexander would not have visited her, they would not have fallen in love, and we would not now be choosing and paying for these terribly expensive hats to go with our excessively costly dresses and jackets, and our even more extravagant shoes.'

'How much was the golden fish worth, finally?' Janice had put off asking this, but now that Mrs Plummer had paid for everything, and they were walking along with handfuls of hat boxes and large shopping bags that announce their expensive designers in very small lettering, she could not resist knowing just *how much*.

'I wouldn't like to tell you, Janice, it's too unbelievable. Gregor believes that next to the painting discovered by the kitchen door that went for millions, this is the most unbelievable discovery. The fish, my fish that Gregor gave me all those years ago because he could not afford to pay me, is such a rare object that a private collector was willing to pay enough to keep me, and Gregor, and you, and all of us for the rest of our days in crespoline, martini, nougatini, and any other teenies that our hearts desire.' Mrs Plummer rolled her eyes dramatically. For a second Janice felt disappointed, and then she realized that Mrs Plummer would never tell her just how much she had received because it would spoil everything. So much better just to be happy, and not to know.

'The young will have their wedding, we will have our happiness, and we will still be able to stroke the golden fish, in our minds,' Mrs Plummer announced as they walked on, Janice clutching her arm, bubbling over with feelings of spring, even though it was summer. 'Because that is what the golden fish is all about, Janice dear. He is about faith, hope, and finally, he turned out to be about charity too.' She smiled, and shook her head. 'And as for that portrait that poor Gregor did of me, it was terrible. So some good has come out of a bad painting at last!'

Coulda, Woulda, Shoulda

Claudia Carroll

CLAUDIA CARROLL was born in Dublin, where she still lives. Her last book, *Remind Me Again Why I Need a Man?* has been bought by Fox TV in the USA for a six part series and the film rights to her latest book, *I Never Fancied Him Anyway*, available as a Transworld Ireland paperback in September, have also been sold. Claudia is single and both titles come from phrases she frequently finds herself using, particularly after rubbish dates. She is currently hassling the producers to give her a walk-on extra part in the movie and isn't a bit fussy what she plays, just as long as they let her keep the clothes. Claudia's new novel, *Do You Want to Know a Secret?*, will be published in Ireland in August and in the UK early in 2009.

O scar Wilde once said that the tragedy of ageing isn't that you're old, it's that you're young. And guess what? Today, I'm discovering exactly what he meant.

It's my fortieth birthday and I'm not a happy woman. Yes, yes, of course, I know that life is way too short to dwell on every bump in the road and that we shouldn't measure our happiness against other people's but . . . well, it's just on this of all days, I can't help but feel deeply unfulfilled, stuck in a rut, and don't even get me started on my love life, which seems to have gone from a slump to an all-out strike.

Finally forty. Officially old enough to know that there's more to life than sex, shoes and parties, but still young enough to know that they *are* the best bits. And that lately I've been seeing damn all of any of them.

'Oh for God's sake, would you just listen to me,' I say out loud, even though I'm alone, in a vague attempt to snap myself out of this pity-fest. My 'surprise' birthday party started half an hour ago and here I am, still in my flat, still only half-dressed and still bloody whingeing. I mean, yes, OK I may have reached this milestone age without a) having a husband/partner/boyfriend/any combination of these three or b) having kids and a family of my own, but I haven't exactly been sitting at home filing my nails all these years, have I? I've . . . erm . . . well, loads to be thankful for. Great friends for starters. And a job I love. And a wonderful family. Yes, OK, I wish my darling Dad was still with us, but Mum's doing great and well, compared to a lot of people, I've loads to be grateful for. Loads. I mean, I could be cleaning out sewers in Calcutta for a living, couldn't I? Then I'd really have something to moan about.

So what's my birthday wish? I can't help asking, while simultaneously shoehorning myself into my old, reliable 'serial result' LBD.

The answer hits me more sharply than a chilli finger poked into my eye. Life, I decide, lashing on the lip gloss, is a bit like Van Morrison's *Moondance* album; all the best bits are on the first side and so, on this of all days . . . I wish . . . I wish . . .

I'm rudely interrupted by a taxi's horn blaring from two floors below. Mandy, my oldest and bestest friend, here to give me a lift to the party and thankfully a good half hour late, as usual. OK, three things you need to know about Mandy.

She's been my best mate ever since school, all the way through college and like I always say, men may come and go, blue eyeliner and the bubble perm may come and go, but true friends are like the Manolo sling back or the Hermès Birkin bag . . . here to stay whether we like it or not.

Her dream was always to become an actress and at aged twenty-one she turned down a place at RADA to accept a tiny part in a daytime soap. She struck it lucky, the character took off and within one season of the show she was a household name, with all the supermarket-opening and tabloid baiting which that entails. But, although she made a lot of money, the show was unexpectedly axed and as she turned thirty, work dried up literally overnight, the way it does for any actress during those death years.

None of the above is helped by the fact that, after almost ten years of virtual unemployment, her name keeps cropping up on those 'Where are they now?' type shows. Pisses her off no end. That, plus the fact that the last gig she was offered was a rip-off of those reality celebrity type shows where you live in the jungle for three weeks eating slugs while Ant and Dec laugh at you. Poor old Mandy, there are times when you really do have to feel sorry for her.

'Happy birthday,' she offers as I clamber in beside her, a bit half-heartedly, but then, she has to face this awful nightmare of turning forty in a few weeks' time and I reckon she's starting to get a bit jittery, and is looking at me now in much the same way that miners look at budgies going down coal shafts.

'So, how does it feel?' she asks, looking at me worriedly.

'Honestly?'

'The truth and nothing but.'

'Fabulous. Turning forty is absolutely, without doubt, the single best thing that ever happened to me.'

She gives me this wry, sideways-on look that she reserves for any time I'm talking total and utter crap.

'Never go on the witness protection programme, Kate, you are *the* worst liar alive.'

'Right then, game's up,' I sigh. 'In that case, today is possibly the most depressing day of my entire life. Right up there with Dad's funeral.'

'Oh now come on, it's just another year, just another milestone, what's so bad?'

'Mandy, as you of all people know only too well,' I say, turning to face her in the back of the taxi, 'that over the years, I've invested a lot of time and energy worrying about stuff that never even happened. Things like, I dunno . . . will I ever be able to afford my own home? Will I be successful and actually make any money? But never, in my wildest dreams did I even think to worry about the fact that I'd end up forty years of age and *alone*. And it's too late to do anything about it now. If love and happiness were meant for me, surely they'd have happened before now?'

'Oh come on, hon, you've got a fabulous job that you love and you're shit hot at. And far better to be on your own than with some jerk who'll only mess you around . . . who needs that? Just look at my pathetic life. I'm seriously facing up to the fact that if I ever want to play any part even approximating my own age group again, I'll have to have a facelift. Bloody Botox, that's raised the bar for all of us and now for any actress to play thirties, you have to look young enough to get ID'd in bars.'

Ageism, I should mention, is a particularly sore point with Mandy, even more so since her agent told her that the only job offers she's likely to get this year are 'third prostitute from the left' type roles in crappy old cop-operas.

'But on the plus side,' I retaliate, 'you did make a fortune on that soap and you've a stunning apartment to show for it *and* you have a fella. Look at me, at forty, I finally have to gracefully accept that I am a man-repeller and that there appears to be something fundamentally unmarriable about me . . .'

'Absolutely untrue. OK, so maybe Mr Right hasn't shown up yet . . .'

'Or maybe he did, years ago, only I was too young and stupid to recognize him.'

'At least you have a proper, decent career that's going from strength to strength,' Mandy interrupts in the 'whose life is worst' contest that's now developed between us. 'May I remind you that aged twenty-one, like the roaring eejit that I am, I turned down a place at RADA so I could be in possibly the worst soap ever committed to the screen.'

'You didn't think that at the time. And you made a fortune out of it. I mean, just look at you. Every stitch you wear is Prada and you always look divine.'

'What I'm trying to say is that if I had gone to RADA, I could be Helen Mirren by now. Or Judi Dench. Instead of thinking myself lucky to get offered guest appearances on any old quiz show that'll have me . . .'

'You have a boyfriend, who'll be on your arm when your turn comes to the medieval torture of having to face your fortieth birthday party. You'll have someone to take you home and help you nurse your hangover the next day. You know what I just realized as you arrived to pick me up?'

'Shoot.'

'That if I had my time over I would do things so differently. Re-prioritize. Not focus on work so much and really, actively go looking for my life partner . . .'

'But you love your job! You're one of the best producers in the business!'

'I know, and I'm grateful but it's just that . . .'

'Is this about James Watson again?'

'No, of course not, it's just that . . .'

I'm making a pretty rubbish job of trying to explain myself, but what I'm really trying to say is that . . . I have twenty-three-year-olds working for me who, when they were handing over the helium birthday balloons today, were looking at me with pity. And I can see what they're thinking. "Yes, you may have a great career and plenty of money but here you are, forty and alone, and that doesn't make you any kind of role model for us."

'I wish I was twenty-one again,' I trail off, lamely. 'Believe me, I would do things so differently. And it's nothing to do with James Watson, honestly."

Although, if I'm being really honest, it kind of is.

OK, I should explain. James was my first boyfriend, my first proper, real true love and I broke up with him because, at twenty-one, I was offered a production trainee course at the BBC, which meant moving to London. Yes, I probably could have kept seeing him and made a go of things, but I didn't. I went for the clean-break option. Like the eejit that I was, I figured there has to be someone better out there for me and guess what? Turns out there wasn't.

'Speaking of wishing you could do things differently . . .' Mandy mutters as the taxi pulls up outside the tennis club where we're having the party.

'What are you talking about?' I ask, but instantly shut up when I see.

It's Sophie. Our other oldest and bestest mate. Or, as everyone seems to refer to her behind her back, 'poor Sophie.' She's just pulled her car in ahead of us, shoved her feet out the driver's door to whip off her trainers and is putting on her party shoes, looking even more frazzled and exhausted than usual, God love her. OK, two things you need to know about her.

The Sophie standing in front of us now is about as different from the Sophie we knew as teenagers as it's possible to get. In fact, looking at her now, it's hard to remember a time when she was wild and mad and up for anything, divilment never far from her sparkling blue eyes as she'd do something really bold, then dare me to do exactly the same. She used to have long red hair down to her bum and smoked from about the age of twelve and never once got caught, whereas all I'd have to do was put one foot out of line to end up with a month's detention. Every guy I knew fancied Sophie, they couldn't not, she was just so much fun and so reckless; even sitting on the top of a bus with her was an adventure. I still have the school yearbook where she was voted 'girl most likely to do absolutely anything.'

'The girl most likely to do absolutely anything' got pregnant at twenty-one and a year later gave birth to my beautiful god-daughter, Ella. By twenty-two, she'd married Ella's dad, a sound engineer called Dave Edmond, and by thirty she had four kids, all under the age of ten. Now she's a divorced single mum, who works part-time in Tesco and really struggles to make ends meet, while her ex-husband has just begun a new relationship with a student beauty therapist from Poland with naturally blonde hair and legs up to her armpits. ('A *student* beauty therapist?' Sophie snarled behind her back. 'For God's sake, what is there to study? How to rub cream into people's faces?')

Poor Sophie. Compared with her, me and Mandy are living in Euro Disney.

'I've never needed a drink so badly in my life,' she sighs, as we all hug and air kiss her. 'If you knew the jigs and reels I had to go through with babysitters just to get out the door tonight. Never, ever have kids, ladies, and if you feel the urge to reproduce, just borrow one of mine for a weekend and you'll be cured. Pure, visual contraception that's what they are. I should charge people.'

The party is in the same tennis club where I've had all my major birthdays before, twenty-first, thirtieth, and now the big four-oh. All courtesy of Mum, who's been on the committee ever since the year dot. She's just inside the door of the function room, handing out vol-au-vents and looking flustered, but she instantly switches to a frown when she sees us arrive.

'Ah, the birthday girl!' she says in a tone of voice that might as well have 'finally!' tacked on to the end of it. 'Half an hour late, dear, nearly all the crudités are gone. And is that really the only thing you had to wear? Oh never mind, at least you're here now and we can start serving the canapés. Look, everyone, she's arrived!'

I glance around the room, and it's so packed that it makes me doubly glad to have Mandy and Sophie on hand.

'SURPRISE!' people call out, and I have to remind myself to act shocked, so end up slapping my hand across my mouth, in an 'I can't believe you all went to this much trouble' gesture, although I'm sure I must look like some rubbishy actor in a B movie.

Most people here are family, cousins mainly, or distant friends who I'm almost embarrassed to see it's so long since we've been in touch, or else Mum's tennis pals. All married, all with kids and all with far better things to do, I'm certain, than sit around here drinking warm white wine and eating mini sausage rolls, listening to a DJ whose idea of good music is to play *Now That's What I Call Music 287*.

'Do the rounds, and we'll get you a very large glass of Sancerre,' Mandy whispers in my ear, bless her. So off I go, shaking the hands, doing the rounds and thanking all and sundry for turning out. Hours must pass, because the next thing I know, a cake is being wheeled out, the DJ is playing 'Happy Birthday' and . . . oh my God, I do not believe this. There are forty candles on the cake. Forty.

'I'll need help with this,' I hiss at Mandy and Sophie, 'otherwise there's a danger I'll need a fire extinguisher.'

'Make a wish!' someone calls out from the back of the bar.

'Easy,' I say, grabbing on to the girls who are flanking me, one right and one left. 'I wish I was twenty-one again.'

'I'll second that,' says Mandy. 'My God, if I was that age again, I could choose to go to RADA, maybe be on the West End by now . . .'

'Oh God, what wouldn't I give to be twenty-one again!' Sophie interrupts. 'Never to have heard the bloody name Dave Edmond . . . I'm telling you ladies, I would have surprised you all and been such a career gal . . .'

You should just see us. Honestly, we're like the Holy Trinity of Coulda, Woulda and Shoulda.

Then, before I know what's even happening, my two strapping, rugby-playing cousins have abandoned their wives and are over to me, pulling me on to the dance floor and telling everyone to stand by while they give me the birthday bumps.

Oh God, I do not believe this. Every major birthday of my life this pair do this to me and I hate it. I politely ask/beg them not to, but they're having none of it. By now I'm screaming at the pair of them over Cliff Richard belting out 'Congratulations,' but it's too late. Next thing they've whooshed me up in the air, bumped me off the ground, and not very gently I might add, then I'm airborne again, screeching for all I'm worth and hating every second of this. From a weird, upside down perspective, I can see Mandy and Sophie looking mortified on my behalf and bravely trying to get the lads to stop this bloody torture and then . . .

It all happens in a split second. One of them, who's holding me by the shoulders, accidentally loses his grip, then there's an almighty cracking sound as I whack my head off a table . . . and then I hit the ground. Head first. Then silence.

'Kate love, open your eyes, there's a good girl,' I can hear my mum's voice coming from miles away. 'Come on, you're frightening us.' My head is thumping, pounding, as I try to sit up, but can only flop limply back down again, like a rag doll.

'Get an ambulance,' someone else says, sounding panicky, 'she's concussed.'

My eyes must flicker a bit because then they all start saying, 'No, look, she's grand, come on . . . Kate?' Slowly, very slowly, with my head throbbing so badly I think I might fall back down again, I somehow manage to open my eyes and sit up. Mum is right beside me, holding my hand and . . . looking younger somehow. She's changed her clothes too, which is weird . . . then I see Mandy, who's now wearing this 1980s-looking power suit – huge shoulder pads, the works, with a lot of major backcombing on her hair . . . Sophie's beside her, but looking like the old Sophie, hair down to her bum again and smoking, even though you're not allowed to smoke in here . . .

It's just the strangest thing. Cliff Richard is still singing 'Congratulations' as I sit up, when I notice that I'm wearing different clothes too . . . this disgusting puffball skirt that I haven't worn since . . . since . . .

It's only when I see a banner hanging over the bar that the penny eventually drops. It screams, in bright red lettering, 'Happy Twenty-First, Kate!' But that's not what's bringing tears to my eyes and a big lump to my throat.

There, kneeling right beside me is James Watson. Yes, *the* James Watson, The One Who Got Away, holding my hand and gazing at me worriedly and . . . oh dear God, standing behind him is Dad. My darling dad who died in 2001. Next thing I know, I've sprung to my feet and am hugging the two of them for all I'm worth, telling James what a complete idiot I was to have left him and telling Dad how much I love him, over and over again.

I must look like I'm only a few coupons short of a special offer because Dad turns to me, pint in hand, and says, 'Ah here, love, that knock on your head must be worse then we thought.'

It's like living in the haziest dream you can imagine, except somehow it's real. It's 1989. Really. I asked everyone about fifty times and wouldn't accept it until the receptionist at the tennis club shoved a newspaper with today's date on it right under my nose. And I'm twenty-one again. And I'm going back home to live with my parents. Back to the house I grew up in, long since demolished, back to my old bedroom, which still has, God help me, a poster of Bros on the wall. Half of me knows that I'm unconscious, but I'm still astonished at the accuracy of my subconscious mind. The other half of me thinks, what the hell, I'm probably dead.

Next thing, I'm back in my old university canteen, and it's just as I remember it, right down to the formica tables and the crap, watery coffee. But I don't care. Because James is sitting beside me, holding my hand and I'd forgotten just how lovely it is to have a proper boyfriend. 'So, you're really turning down that job offer at the BBC?' he's asking me, stunned.

'Absolutely, no question,' I say, firmly.

'You'd actually do that for me?' he asks, looking at me like he's waiting for the 'but'.

'James, if there's one thing I've learned, it's that *we* come first. You and me.'

And then we kiss and it's divine and I love being this young and in love all over again. Every time I go home I hug my dad so much I'm embarrassing him. And as if that wasn't reason enough to dance around the place with sheer joy, I'm back to being a size ten again and I haven't a single wrinkle on my face. Spots yeah, but no saggy boobs or falling bum. *And* I even get to play God with Mandy and Sophie's lives too. I meet them in McDonald's for a coffee (can you believe there's nowhere else to go? When I mentioned Starbucks, everyone just looked at me) and I bossily tell Mandy that she should stop dithering and just accept the place she's been offered at RADA. And when Sophie starts telling us about her new crush who she wants to go 'all the way' with, Dave Edmond, I tell her he's bad news and she should avoid, avoid, avoid.

'Why are you so certain he's going to turn into an asshole?' Sophie asks, pulling on a cigarette and looking at me, puzzled.

'Because. Trust me, I've got a crystal ball.'

Next thing, it's like a hazy fog has drifted over me and

now I can hear Cliff Richard singing 'Congratulations' all over again, which can only mean one thing. I'm back to lying on the floor of the tennis club and back out of this lovely reverie, to being forty again. Except somehow, things aren't quite right. Mandy's beside me, but somehow doesn't look anything like her usual fabulous, glamorous self. And there's no sign of Sophie, which is odd . . .

'What year is it?' I mutter. 'Who's the prime minister? How old am I?'

'You're concussed and I'm taking you to the hospital,' Mandy says firmly.

'Look, I know I sound mental and maybe I am, but please, please tell me what's going on in all our lives. Please, I have to know, it's important.'

She looks at me worriedly, but caves into the mad-woman that I sound like. 'Well, to be honest, hon, I'd have thought tonight would be an opportunity to forget about it all. What with poor Sophie having IVF – you do remember that they've kept her in at the hospital to runs tests to figure out why she's not getting pregnant? You only went to see her yesterday.'

'And what about you?'

'Me? Well, if I don't get a job very soon, there's a good chance I'll end up a bag lady. I can't believe I'm going to be forty in a few weeks and I'm still living in a rented flat with a bunch of drama students and cockroaches.'

'But . . . you went to RADA . . . didn't you?'

'Sure I did. And I can count on the fingers of one hand the amount of jobs I've had since I graduated. To think I turned down a perfectly good, well-paid job in a soap opera just to do some posh acting course there.

I need my head looked into, and judging by the way you're going on, I'm not the only one.'

I'm half afraid to ask my next question, but I know that I have to.

'And what about James?'

She looks at me and I just know by her face that she's terrified to answer.

'Mandy, I really need to know,' I gently help her.

'You really can't remember?'

'Not a thing.'

'You're divorced now, honey. And this morning, on the day of your big birthday, he told you he's getting married again. What an asshole . . . and when I think of what you gave up for him . . .'

I slump back on to the ground, hating this reality, this parallel time that I seem to be stuck in. I didn't mean to, but somehow, by playing God, I've managed to ruin everyone's life, my own included. At least the way things were, I did have a great career. And Mandy had plenty of money and a lovely place to live. And Sophie had four fabulous kids . . . now, because of my meddling, we're all so much worse off . . .

Suddenly I feel nauseous, but just as I think I'm about to gag, my eyes open and now I'm lying on a hospital bed with the girls beside me and Mum perched on a chair at the far end of the room.

'She's back!' Mandy almost screams, gripping my hand. 'Kate, can you hear me? Do you know where you are?'

'You gave us such a fright, dear' says Mum. 'Kept talking all sorts of rubbish about seeing your father again. But the doctor says with rest, you'll be just fine.'

'And then you were having this imaginary

conversation with James Watson,' says Sophie. 'Scary stuff, babe.'

'Sophie, how many kids to you have?' I hiss urgently at her.

'Four,' she shrugs. 'Why, do you wanna adopt one?'

And that's when I know.

I just know that I'm back in my own reality. In 2008. With my two best friends and Mum, the people who matter most to me.

'We're all so lucky,' is all I can say in a weak whisper, before slumping back on to the pillow.

We mightn't have thought so, but we all made the right choices along the way. And everything's fine. It just might take me another forty years to explain it, that's all . . .

The Man Shortage

Kathy Lette

KATHY LETTE first achieved *succès de scandale* as a teenager, with the novel *Puberty Blues*. After several years as a newspaper columnist and television sitcom writer in America and Australia, she wrote the internationally bestselling *Girls Night Out, The Llama Parlour, Foetal Attraction, Mad Cows, Altar Ego, Nip 'n' Tuck,* and *Dead Sexy*. Her latest bestseller is *How To Kill Your Husband – and other handy household hints.* Kathy Lette's new novel, *To Love, Honour and Betray (Till Divorce Us Do Part)*, will be published by Bantam Press in September. She lives in London with her husband and two children. Visit her website at www.kathylette.com

ooking back, I blame the man shortage. All the men were either married or gay. Or married *and* gay. And the rest had a three grunt vocabulary of 'na', 'dunno', and 'ergh.' By twenty-five I was a relationships limbo dancer – my expectations just kept getting lower and lower. For three months I went out with a man whose tattoos were probably his only reading material. I finally left him over his grammar. 'I brung you this drink'. My next boyfriend was a surfie. Addicted to Leonard Cohen and Sartre, I preferred to surf my brain waves. Put it this way, he only used the word 'opera' next to the word 'soap.' He thought 'erudite' was some kind of glue. I soon swapped him for a rock star. I tried to overlook the fact that the man's culinary highlight was a dip enhancer – chutney or tomato sauce. He thought that cheese was nothing more than butter gone bad. On our two-month anniversary I took him to a French restaurant to celebrate. He responded by pointing out loudly that just because the French gave snails a fancy name like 'escargot' didn't mean you weren't eating pond life. He said that French cuisine was just where they 'serve everythin' in pools of congealed phlegm . . . Garçon, can we have a snail and a frog in a mosquito marinade?'

I lost my appetite for him after that. But a month of celibacy in social Siberia and I started to worry that I was forever doomed to wear full make-up and high-rise heels to the supermarket – just in case I met someone . . .

But then I did meet someone. Dan. He had a Casanova grin which was all impish insolence. There was also a tousled tenderness beneath his bad boy bravado – a cryptic sadness which I couldn't quite decipher. The man possessed a perfection which inclined observers towards the adjectival. Women who were unused to superlatives had to tilt their heads backwards so that their eyeballs wouldn't fall out. He was emotionally articulate, a doctor and could give dance lessons to Michael Jackson. The dancing was as dirty as you could get without latex. He was one in a million – an eligible heterosexual man in full-time employment. It was a wonder he hadn't been stripped down and sold for parts. With Dan's chiselled good looks and prime pectoral real estate (the man had serious pecs appeal), at first I presumed that he was way out of my league. But he seemed to enjoy my company – and he wanted a lot of it. Opera, theatre, ballet, galleries, restaurants – after a month of fun and frivolity, I felt sure I had found my Duke of Right.

Best of all, he didn't want to rush me. After a scintillating night at the opera and supper it was so late he suggested I stay at his flat. 'We could just sleep. I promise nothing will happen, Cara. I won't touch you.'

I looked at him dubiously. I'd had enough experience with men to know that this is what they always say – and then all night there's the insistent prod of his appendage in the small of your back.

But I awoke next morning, unmolested. The fact that Dan respected me for my brain and not my body only endeared him to me more. It endeared him to me so much that I wanted to express my feelings physically. I now *wanted* to discover the supple hydraulics of my boyfriend's manhood. Women need love! Ask any syndicated advice columnist.

Yes, it was time to play Doctor. I wanted to be reckless, impulsive, Caligulaesque. Those Roman emperors would have nothing on me. Bring on the fatted calves. And not those things above my socks either. Why, I wondered, couldn't females just give in to raw uncomplicated desire? I wanted to be guilty of Acute Lust in the First Degree. I stayed at his place again – but this time it was Dan who woke with the imprint of my erect nipples in *his* back.

While Dan was showering I cast a critical eye over my naked body in the bedroom mirror. I obviously possessed the sexual magnetism of a half-thawed rissole. Perhaps I needed to become more erotic? A magazine article suggested a Brazilian wax ... But believe me, that may sound erotic, but when it's growing back it looks like a shag pile that's been terrorized. Besides which, Dan preferred to wax lyrical. Content in each other's company, we talked and talked until our lips dropped off.

But it was about now that I began to have my first twinges of doubt. Most unsettling was his half-hearted kissing. Making the face of a child rejecting spinach, he would dodge my lips and make minimal contact with my left earlobe. Not to mention his taste in movies – *Maurice* and *The Way We Were*. Worst of all, I seemed to be flying right under his R-rated radar. Dan was so gorgeous he could excite passion in a large geological formation. He was a sex object all right – I wanted sex and he objected to it. His excuse was that his triathlon training left him physically exhausted. But it was hard to just 'cuddle on the couch' when my libido had grown into the size of Paraguay.

But as Dan was perfect in every other way (the man was so handsome my girlfriends thought I'd found him in a male order catalogue) I overlooked these slight misgivings. Instead I leapt on to him as though he were the last helicopter out of Saigon.

And so we became a couple. His mother adored me but his friends did not. I spent so many fascinating nights at parties, watching bowls of guacamole turn black as his mates studiously ignored me.

My girlfriends pinpointed the truth about Dan long before I did. 'It's a Ken and Ken kind of situation, Cara,' one pal hinted, during a heart to heart.

'Your boyfriend is a middle order batsman *for the other side*,' another added, euphemistically.

'He has effete of clay', prompted my punster pal.

'He's sailing up the windward passage,' another asserted, adding in desperation, 'The man leaves no buttock unturned.'

Finally my sister confessed that she'd actually seen Dan picking up a guy at the local public swimming pool.

But even then I defended him. 'You're wrong. The only thing Dan's ever picked up at that pool is athlete's foot.'

My best girlfriend put on her Madame Defarge face as she watched, gimlet eyed, from the sidelines. 'Well don't say I didn't warn you . . . he'll break your heart.'

'In my opinion, advice is like syphilis,' I retorted haughtily. 'It's better to give than to receive.'

When I confronted Dan about the rumours, he explained that he'd been so overworked at the hospital and so wound up of late that he needed to go away for a week or two to sort himself out. He kissed me tenderly at the airport, swearing his devotion – and headed off for Bali.

I surreptitiously followed, to surprise him. But Dan didn't enjoy the surprise as much as I'd anticipated. Lounging by the hotel pool, I tried to engage him in our usual witty banter. But after one hour of conversation, tropical sun lounger hostilities were rivalling two Balkan republics. From disco to dining room, from beach to bistro, my feelings of failure grimly dogged me. Not even Michael Palin could turn this journey into an amusing anecdote.

When I complained that he was ignoring me, Dan announced that he had come on holiday to find himself . . . Backing off, I let him go out alone, but stalked him relentlessly to every club in town. At twenty-six, I was hoping to never again attend loud discos full of sherbet-eyeshadowed teenage girls and their scrofulous, shaggy-haired male companions, dancing like things in pain, curling and coiling and jumping from foot to foot without a defined side parting in sight. But Dan seemed to adore it. And I soon found out why. From my hiding place behind various pot plants, I noted my boyfriend's concupiscent glance towards the other boys on the dance floor. The clubs were full of young handsome men, thin as skittles. And it was Dan who bowled them over.

I smiled until my face cramped and my teeth wanted to fall out.

Dan had come away to find himself. But what he found instead was a gay towel attendant called Norbert. My heart flopped like a pole-vaulter into a mattress. I was so in love with Dan by now that I seriously considered a ménage à trois. At least it would give me a chance to practise my French accent, I rationalized. And wouldn't it be useful to have two men around to fix fuses and change car tyres?

For a few days my mind sort of sat on its hands. OK, so maybe my boyfriend was coming out, but couldn't I just push him back in again? I got so depressed at the thought of losing his witty, wisecracking company that I took up smoking. For a non-smoker I seemed to be about to wrest the World Nicotine-Ingestion Record from the beagle community.

'I can change him. I can! I can convert him!' I said to my girlfriends over endless cappuccinos.

'Oh my God, Cara. What's that noise?' my best friend replied. 'Oh I know. It's the sound of millions of women laughing themselves to death.'

The person you go out with says a lot about you. Going out with a male you hadn't realized is gay says that you are a complete bloody idiot. But cutting Dan out of my life would be a lot like having root canal surgery – only more painful.

Still, a boyfriend-ectomy was unavoidable. In the end I just couldn't bear to have sex with a man when I knew we'd both be fantasizing about the same person (Tom Cruise).

I was obviously holding the World Indoor Record for Self-Delusion. If I'm honest, the real reason I'd failed to notice that my boyfriend made Liberace seem straight was because of my dread of having to hastily organize another girls' night out on Valentine's Day. I was obviously going to have to master the Kama Sutra for One. Just when I was thinking that I'd declare myself a conscientious objector in the sex war and devote myself to a future of staying in every night tweezing odd stray facial hairs, Dan thought it would be a good idea to introduce me to his brother. Michael was home on holiday from his banking job in Europe.

There are a number of props which increase sexual arousal, particularly in women. Chief among these is a man with an apartment in Paris. Oh, it also helped that he was a perfect carbon copy of his brother. Michael was so physically perfect; I suspected he'd been inflated by blowing into his toe. We're talking the kind of pneumatic buttocks which had done more for female masturbation than Doctor Ruth. When he spoke to any woman, she would make a noise not unlike someone forced to chew her own foot off. When I met him, I smiled so hard I pulled a muscle.

In only one respect did the brothers differ. Michael was a hot-to-trot heterosexual. And in between girl-friends. I knew the romance wasn't going to last, but Michael broke my sexual drought in the most spectacular way. Happy? Hormonal Houston, we have lift off! It also helped me forgive Dan. He was obviously so much happier out of the closet. And, after I got over the heartache, we eventually became even better friends. So, I guess that's the moral of the story – be true to yourself. Better latent than never . . .

*A Million Love
Songs*

ANITA
NOTARO

When ANITA NOTARO decided to quit a job she loved as a TV Producer in 2002 her boss sent her to see a shrink. Thankfully, today she's still reasonably sane and enjoying a new career as a writer more than she ever believed possible. *Take a Look at Me Now*, her fourth novel, went to No. 1 on the Irish Bestseller List and won The Galaxy Popular Fiction Book of the Year at the 2008 Irish Book Awards. It will be available as a Transworld Ireland paperback in November.

When she misses the glamour of television she works as a freelance director on Ireland's top rated soap *Fair City* and travels to exotic locations for the holiday programme *No Frontiers*. Otherwise it's sweat pants and too many chocolate biscuits as she tackles her fifth novel.

'And that was "How Do You Keep The Music Playing" – today's choice in our Lively Listeners' Loveboat Lunchtime Lesson.' The radio DJ was vomit smooth. Carla could just picture him – mid-fifties, beer belly, medallion, dyed hair. She despised him and his programme, it was for fuddy-duddies and she was thirty-eight. Actually, she was thirty-eight feeling seventy-eight and that was part of the problem.

'So go on, admit it, you danced around the kitchen, smooching as you swept . . .' the oral equivalent of a video nasty droned on, until Carla could no longer stomach it. She normally never listened to this station, it was for pensioners. But lately she'd started to enjoy their morning news programme and she was just too lazy to turn it off. Now the idiotic presenter of the worst programme she'd ever heard had got under her skin. He was always dispensing ridiculous bits of advice such as 'a clean wife is more important than a clean floor' or 'a good dinner is lovely but a good kiss keeps you lively.' Ugh. This morning it was 'a dab of perfume is worth a hundred logs on the fire.' The relentless schmaltz, combined with some of the naffest songs she'd ever heard, made Carla decide she'd had enough. Reaching over, she yanked the plug from the wall and turned on her CD player, dismissing the thought that perhaps all that unwanted advice was a bit too close to home these days.

For lunch Carla had an avocado salad which was the

exact colour of her mother's bathroom suite, and as appetizing as she suspected munching on the plastic toilet seat would be. God, she'd hated every second of WeightWatchers today. But as she chucked the soggy mess into the bin she knew it had been a long time since she loved anything about her life.

After that, it was a day full of ferrying – rugby and piano and shopping and sports practice – another element of her life that Carla loved and hated in equal measure. She hated the routine and loved the neediness of the kids, thirteen-year-old twins Sophie and Sean. But even that was diminishing rapidly. They were branching out so fast it scared her and letting them go was shaping up to be a big issue for her, she could feel it as sure as if she was already in therapy.

At seven she got a text from her husband Matt.

Don't hold food for me. This meeting looks like it's dragging on. I'll have a sandwich here. X

Determined not to start reading anything into it, Carla pulled the casserole out of the oven and yelled 'Dinner' in the general direction of the stairs, provoking action of a kind only equalled every time she opened her purse.

'You OK, Mum?' Sophie asked it a lot these days.

'Fine, darling. How was school today?'

'I need money for the school outing,' Sean was on form. He started to eat and text one of his thousand closest friends at the same time. With huge aqua eyes that startled everyone he met, he was the image of his father and just about as popular.

'Sean, you know the rules, no mobiles at the table—' she began to lecture as she always seemed to be doing these days. Something about wanting to fight with his father, she knew deep down, and taking it out on him instead.

'Sorry,' he capitulated immediately with that endearing grin and Carla felt even more guilty.

She was in bed when Matt got home.

'Sorry, couldn't get rid of the clients,' he mumbled, kissing her on the head and rolling over. He'd phoned her a couple of times, it was what he did these days.

Within seconds he was snoring and Carla did what she always seemed to do these days, turned over and watched him sleeping and tried to make sense of it all. He was still one of the most attractive men she'd ever met, but then she'd always known that, didn't need the battery of friends and colleagues who told her so constantly. And in her heart she knew he was nice inside as well as out.

Next morning, Matt stirred before six, in preparation for a two-day trip to London. Carla got up with him, just as she'd done for years.

'So, where are you staying?' she asked casually, pouring coffee and trying not to sound as if she was interrogating him. During one of their many arguments lately he'd told her she sometimes made him feel claustrophobic.

'Usual,' he said. 'It's central and they do twenty-four-hour room service, so I can just chill out and watch TV once I finish.' He bit into a slice of toast and swallowed his coffee, standing as he always did, mind already far away from her, she suspected.

'You look tired, are you OK?' he asked now, contradicting her thoughts.

'Why does everyone keep asking me that? I'm fine.'

'Have you a lot on today?'

'Playing taxi . . . nothing much,' she trailed off, feeling inadequate.

'Well, I think you should take a bit of time out for yourself, have a massage or something,' he was checking his BlackBerry as he spoke.

'Won't help I'm afraid.' She was flippant but her tone was clipped. She felt, rather than saw him stop in his tracks and knew he was staring at her back.

He let out a breath, as if contemplating whether to say anything or not. 'Right, I'd better head.' Matt came up behind Carla and turned her towards him, searching her face. 'Anything I can do?'

'Nope.' She wasn't about to cry in front of him. Not again.

'Mind yourself. I'll call you as soon as I finish work, and I'm on the mobile all day if you need me.' He was reassuring her and they both knew it.

She watched him stroll out into the spring sunshine, looking like someone you'd wonder about if you saw him on the street. Without letting herself brood, Carla raced up the stairs and turned on the shower, determined to be out somewhere when he called home this evening to talk to the three of them.

At the school she eyed up the other mothers, knowing she didn't really fit in with her peers. They all looked identical – blow-dried, poker-straight hair and manicured nails – and they wore a uniform of wedge boots, pinafores or long skirts and floaty coats. They were mostly kitted out in shades of grey or black. Oh, and their handbags all had sparkly gold bits or diamonds attached and they drove silver or black patent-leather-shiny gas guzzlers.

Carla had untameable curly hair and was dressed in jeans and a long-sleeved white shirt, her staple. If she deviated at all it was usually to replace the jeans with black trousers for a more formal occasion. Her car was a five-year-old Volvo estate that needed an overhaul as much as she did.

'Your car is paid for by the company,' Matt had urged her the other day. 'You were due an 08 model months ago, what's the problem?'

'I like the car I have,' Carla had no idea why she was being so stubborn.

'You could get leather seats, electric mirrors, the lot,' he cajoled but she shook her head, knowing he was trying to do something nice for her and resisting just because . . . well, just because.

In the car 'yer man' was on again. Today it was 'Here, There And Everywhere' by the Beatles. Before she realized it, Carla was singing along, something about how love never dies. His line today was 'tell your partner at least once a day that you adore him and keep the magic alive'. Yeah right. Annoyed, she changed stations and tried to immerse herself in the death notices being dished out on another local channel, wondering if love had well and truly died for her and Matt. At home, Carla dialled her friend Patricia and they arranged to meet for coffee. Pat insisted it was no trouble to pick her up and as she got into the car *that* voice was still dispensing advice.

'Turn it off, please,' Carla begged.

'Why? I love him,' Pat laughed. 'All those sad songs, they always put me in a good mood.'

'Wall-to-wall sop, one more smarmy than the next,' Carla told her friend, clearly disgruntled.

'Who robbed your rattle, then?'

'I hate that DJ.'

'I love him, he's a hoot. Besides, he's cute, did you see him in the paper today, at that awards thing last night?'

'Cute?' Carla scoffed, sure Pat was mixing him up with someone else. 'I can just picture him, beer belly oozing out over his trousers, hair coiffed, loads of gold fillings and reeking of aftershave.'

''Fraid not, darling,' Pat pulled smoothly into a parking space, 'although I wouldn't have been able to judge the aftershave from the article.' She grinned and reached onto the back seat for her handbag and a newspaper. 'Bit like your man out of *Desperate Housewives*, I'd say.' She threw the tabloid at her friend.

'Don't be ridiculous,' Carla was indignant as she unfolded it. 'But . . .' she stared at the caption. 'That cannot be him, it just can't.'

'That's what it says,' Pat laughed as she got out of the car. 'He can give me tips about my love life any day of the week.'

'But, he's young, he's—'

'Good looking, sexy, I know. That's what I told you.'

'It must be the wrong caption,' Carla stuttered. 'That guy on the radio could be my father. Besides, he's pompous and condescending and . . . straight out of the dark ages.'

'I think it's meant to be tongue in cheek, Carla. Will you chill out, for Pete's sake? What's happened to your sense of fun lately?' Pat instantly regretted saying it, she'd known there was something up for ages, just hadn't a clue what it was, despite a fair bit of prompting.

'Sorry, I didn't mean that,' she said quickly. 'Come

72

on, last one in buys the scones, or is it brown cardboard toast today? I put on a kilo this week.' She made a face at Carla. 'Still, feck it, I need a sugar fix. My treat,' she said by way of a further apology.

After that, they spent an enjoyable hour laughing about diets and moaning about kids and taking bets on the DJ having had a facelift. Apart from that, it was another non-eventful day.

'Hey guys, I'm going for a run,' she shouted up the stairs at around nine.

Two confused faces poked their heads over the banister. That in itself was unusual, normally at this time of the night they couldn't hear her for the music belting out. Both swore it was the only way they could study.

'A run? But—'

'Cool, we'll be grand,' Sophie cut across her brother, suspecting he was just about to tease their mother. The truth was Carla hadn't jogged in three years and was potential heart attack material if she tried now. But she was determined not to hang around waiting for Matt to call.

'I'm not taking my mobile, it'll only annoy me,' she told them. 'Listen out for the house phone. If Dad rings tell him I'll probably jump straight into the bath so I'll talk to him tomorrow.'

'Right so,' Sean still looked dopey-boy confused, but he settled for another 'You OK?'

'Yes,' she sighed. 'Now will you please all stop asking me that every five minutes? See you later and remember, don't answer the door while I'm out.' Carla made no attempt to run, even down the gentle slope of the driveway, settling into a stride instead and listening to Norah Jones on her iPod.

'Dad rang,' was the greeting on her return. 'Sean told him you were out, but I warned him not to say you were jogging, in case he got worried.' Sophie looked like she thought she'd said the wrong thing. Why were the three of them tiptoeing around her all the time lately? It made Carla feel like an invalid.

'What I mean is, he might have been worried about you out in the dark on your own.' Her daughter tried to cover herself.

'As opposed to worried about whether I'd come home in an ambulance,' Carla smiled. 'It's OK love, I know what you meant.'

Sophie looked relieved. 'You, er, want me to make you some hot chocolate?'

'Yes, that'd be great. I'm going to run the bath.'

'Dad said to tell you he's just arrived back at the hotel and that he's in room 601 if you need him and can't get through on the mobile.'

'OK, thanks. I won't bother ringing in case he's dozing on the bed. I'll talk to him in the morning.'

'You could always send him a smoochy text?' Sophie wasn't letting it go tonight for some reason.

'I could, you're right.' But I won't, she didn't add.

Next morning, amid the usual chaos, Carla forgot to ring Matt. She was just about to leave home when he phoned.

'How's it going?'

'Fine, I was just heading for the shops.'

'What did you get up to last night? The kids said you'd just gone out when I phoned.'

'Nothing much. Went for a run, then—' It was out before she realized.

'You? Jogging? That's a new one.'

'Well, have to keep fit in case I get a new man.' Carla had no idea why she'd said that, it seemed like she was always trying to hurt him these days. 'Hang on while I turn down that blasted radio,' she said quickly in an effort to change the subject. 'I hate that bloody DJ . . .' She moved across the room with the phone in her hand.

'What's that song?' Matt asked, surprising her. He was normally a million miles away during these calls.

Carla knew it well. It was part of the soundtrack of one of her favourite movies.

' "It Must Have Been Love," ' she mumbled.

'Isn't that the one you always sing so beautifully when you're cleaning the bathroom?' he asked, tongue glued to his cheek, Carla guessed.

'As opposed to your melodious rendition of that whiny Leonard Cohen song, what's it called?' Carla smiled. It felt odd to be sharing a joke with him.

' "I'm Your Man." '

'Yeah, well . . .' There was nothing to say to that really.

'Am I still your man, Carla?' Matt asked quietly.

'I dunno, are you?' she asked quietly back. At that moment someone called his name in the background.

'Sorry, Carla, I've got to go, Bob Condren from Island Pictures has just arrived to pick me up.' He hesitated. 'Listen, it looks like I'll have to be here for the weekend.' He sounded strained. 'The clients from Singapore are staying and Gerry and I—'

'What?' Carla couldn't believe her ears. 'But I thought we might—' She clamped her mouth shut, determined not to let him hear her disappointment. It only served to remind her of how important he was in her life, something she didn't want to think about.

'Fine,' she said through tight lips. 'I'll talk to you later.'

'Listen, let me call you back in a sec—'

'Bye.' She hung up and put her head in her hands, wondering where it would all end.

'. . . and our Lovers' Request today is a real golden oldie.' Carla heard that voice again. It was worse now that she knew he was young and sexy and probably had a hundred women in tow.

'I hate you, you're a moron,' Carla spat at the radio as she scraped back her chair.

'It's called 'If Ever I Would Leave You' and it's especially for . . .' But Carla didn't hear any more. She slumped back down at the kitchen table and began to cry, and once she started it was as if someone had unblocked a drain in her heart. It was that song. Her father used to sing it to her mother. Something about not being able to leave in summer, or winter, or any other season. She wondered if Matt had ever thought of leaving her. It was her worst fear.

She was still sitting there, eyes rimmed in scarlet when the twins burst in. She'd forgotten they were finishing school early today.

'Mum, what's wrong?' Sean asked in a panicky voice.

'Are you feeling sick?' Sophie dropped her bag and knelt down beside her.

'No, I'm sorry. I'm fine, really.'

'Please tell us what's wrong?'

'Nothing, I promise.' Carla blew her nose and decided she had to pull herself together. 'It's just that song,' she shook her head. 'It reminded me of Mum. Dad used to sing it to her whenever they had a row,' Carla tried to smile.

'I knew it had to be serious. You never cry.' Sean seemed relieved.

'I'm sorry, Mum. We should have been more sensitive.' It hurt Carla to hear her daughter shouldering another upset. 'It's only six months since Nana died . . .' Carla knew her daughter was right.

'Thanks, love.' She patted Sophie's arm. 'It is still a bit raw . . .' But these days it hurt more when she thought about her and Matt.

'Do you want to go to the grave? That'll cheer you up,' Sean asked, and mother and daughter looked at each other before bursting out laughing.

'What planet do you occupy?' Sophie was ready to throttle her twin.

'Sorry,' Sean looked goofy. 'What I mean is, you like digging it up and planting things, don't you?' He was all male confusion.

'Yes, I do, but not today, thanks.' Carla ruffled his hair.

'Well, I'll go whenever you want, I can carry that foul-smelling rotten stuff you put on it.' Sean ambled away, happy he'd played his part.

'That would be your home-made compost, Mum.' Sophie was still smiling. 'Will I make us some tea?'

'Yes, please.' She made a long-overdue decision to try and move on. 'I'm going to do my groceries online today, I think, and spend an hour shopping for something new for myself in that new boutique in Dundrum you told me about.'

'Great. Want me to come with you?' Sophie asked as she filled the kettle.

'No thanks, I'll ring Debbie.' Her sister was just the tonic she needed right now. 'And I think I'll treat myself to a facial.' Carla decided it was time she started looking after herself again.

'Fab. Ring them now.'

As it happened the salon she liked couldn't take her till Monday, but Sophie made her book it anyway, even though Carla thought getting her hair done and having a facial on a weekday was a waste.

'Dad'll be home on Monday.' Sophie winked at her. 'He always notices when you do something different or buy some new clothes.'

Used to, Carla's thoughts went the usual way, but she cut them off.

'In fact, he was asking me if maybe we'd all go out together one night next week for a pizza. Could we? It's ages since we've done anything like that.' Carla noted the careful way her daughter asked, and wondered if she knew something wasn't right, despite their best efforts.

'Maybe,' was the best she could muster.

'Shame to waste that new hairdo.' Her daughter tried harder.

'We'll see.'

'Great. I'll text Dad.'

Matt phoned several times over the weekend but each time he tried to talk to her one of the twins wanted him for something or other. Sean's Bebo page or Sophie's new phone or a computer game they couldn't quite master. Matt was the technical wizard in the family and the kids loved it that their dad knew all the latest gadgets. Their mates all thought he was the coolest father around.

For the rest of the weekend Carla kept herself busy. She threw out half her wardrobe, recycled until there wasn't a bottle or piece of cardboard in the house and even painted the front door when she was tempted to think.

On Monday morning she dropped the kids off and

went for her treatments, feeling lighter in herself as she headed back home.

Turn on your favourite DJ

The text came in from Matt just as she got into the car. Without thinking, she did as instructed. It was the usual, today he was urging listeners to 'never trouble trouble, till trouble troubles you'. Carla grimaced at the ultimate cliché, but maybe that's what she had been doing. Matt had never once mentioned leaving her or the kids and that was the most important thing.

She was still mulling things over in her head when something made her stop and listen. Funny, she thought she'd heard him say Carla and Matt.

Hitting the brake at the red light, Carla also flicked the volume control on the steering wheel.

'So, Carla, your husband Matt just wanted me to tell you that he loves you very much and asked me to play this particular song. He said you'll know what he's trying to say. So here goes, for anyone out there who's had a quarrel, remember that life's very short and sometimes you have to forgive and forget . . .' The drivel tumbled off his tongue but suddenly he didn't sound half as patronizing.

The tears came the instant she heard the intro. Elton John's *Greatest Hits* had always been one of her 'so gross it's almost cool' albums, at least that's how Matt and the kids described it when she used to listen to it every Saturday morning in the old days, back when they were a proper family, before all this had split them wide open.

It was 'Sorry Seems To Be The Hardest Word'. She tried to sing along and bite her lip at the same time. Finally, Carla knew she was ready to forgive Matt for the affair.

Pink Diamond

Jo Rees

JO REES studied English and Drama at Goldsmiths, University of London. She has had various careers including stints in the city, marketing and publishing. She now divides her time between Spain and the UK, where she lives by the sea with her husband and their three daughters. Her new novel, *Platinum*, is now available from Bantam Press.

*A*nya Von Trescow-Myers, sole heiress of the Myers transport and telecommunications fortune, lay on the lounger beside the infinity pool and ran her manicured foot along the tanned, oiled shin of her other impossibly long leg. Two slices of cucumber lay over her eyes as she turned her face up to the early morning Mediterranean sun, as if she didn't have a care in the world.

From the shadows of the art deco pool house of Le Manoir DuChamp, Anya's estate in the South of France, Karen Kydd watched Anya and then glanced anxiously at her Rolex watch, feeling the calfskin dossier containing the pre-nuptial agreement papers starting to get uncomfortably hot under her arm.

She couldn't indulge Anya much longer. It was already ten and Sona, the personal trainer, would be here for Anya's pilates session in a few minutes. And then the ghastly publicist Anya had insisted on hiring to cover tonight's 'little soirée' would descend to discuss the celebrity guest list.

But Karen knew from bitter experience that Anya needed careful handling in the morning. She hadn't gone to bed until at least four a.m., and was almost certainly hungover now, if the empty cocktail glasses on the rooftop terrace were anything to go by.

Karen herself had a million things to do. On top of briefing the florist and chef, she had to finalize the guests' landing schedule with Tom, Anya's private pilot, oversee the arrival of the party planners and then coax Anya into signing these papers. All before lunch.

'OK, OK, I know you're there, KK,' Anya called out, with a sigh.

Karen smiled. She had been Anya's shadow since she'd started working for the young socialite fifteen years ago. They'd met in New York when Karen had taken a summer job in the office of the late Duncan Myers, Anya's terrifying grandfather.

As soon as Karen had entered Anya's orbit, she'd found herself sucked inextricably into her world. A week had stretched into two, then a month. Soon Anya had insisted that Karen dump her plans for college and stay on as Anya's personal assistant. And what Anya wanted, Anya got. She'd upped the salary and benefits, until Karen had no choice but to submit.

Of course, Karen had meant to leave years ago and pursue her own dreams with the money she'd saved. Anya was almost impossible to live with, let alone work for twenty-four seven. She was spoilt and capricious, greedy and yet insatiable, a social chameleon who never stayed still. She'd flit off to a party in Miami at the drop of a hat, or go skiing with friends in Aspen on a Tuesday, only to be in Morocco by the weekend.

But whilst the world's gossip magazines became increasingly fascinated with the elusive party girl, only Karen knew the truth. In Anya, she saw the vulnerable lonely girl who'd been brought up by strict nannies and stuffy private schools.

The one time Karen had threatened to leave her, Anya had begged her to stay. She couldn't leave her, not now, not ever. Who else in the world could Anya trust? How could she survive without Karen? Karen was vital . . . indispensable, she'd wailed. Her only true friend. And

Karen, flattered, unable to bear Anya crying, had buckled. She guessed now she always would. She was too loyal. That was her own weakness. One she couldn't quite seem to overcome.

'I didn't mean to interrupt,' Karen said, as Anya sat up, removing the cucumber from her eyes. Anya grunted and reached across the elegant mosaic table beside her for her giant Dior shades, lifting a glass of iced water to her perfect lips.

Anya quickly swivelled off the lounger, the short towelling robe billowing out behind her, revealing her perfect body in her white bikini, as she sashayed up the steps in her mules. She thrust her hand out to Karen. 'Nails. Natural, or French polished?' she demanded. 'What's going to look better with the Pink?'

'Oh, I think a light polish. Certainly not French,' Karen said. She flipped open her mobile phone. 'I'll get Suzanne down here,' she said, speed-dialling Anya's personal beautician.

The 'Pink' – the subject of Anya's obsession – was the Treblinsky Pink diamond, a stone so valuable and rare that Anya was throwing a party tonight to celebrate its arrival in her life. The pink diamond set in the platinum ring had been in Serge Treblinsky's family since the days of the Russian Tsars. Tonight Serge was going to present it to Anya formally, to replace the 'throw-away' three-carat diamond engagement ring that Anya currently wore on her slim finger.

The Pink. It would finally be here. Karen wondered if she was more excited about seeing it than Anya was. When she'd tried to find out its value from her contacts in the jewellery trade, she'd been stunned by their reaction. Most had never even seen such a rare diamond, let alone been asked to value one for insurance. But they'd all known of the Treblinksy Pink's existence. 'Priceless,' they'd each muttered in the same, reverential whisper.

Serge Treblinsky had strutted into Anya and Karen's lives along the quayside of English Harbour in Antigua the previous Christmas, asking Anya to a party on board his mega-yacht. Karen, who'd been desperate to steer Anya away from her fixation on a junkie rock star, had insisted Anya accept, despite her protestations that Serge was too old and too short.

On the contrary, Karen had thought, charming fifty-year-old Serge was perfect for her. An oligarch's son, educated at Eton, Serge had been a racing driver but now owned a string of galleries. Sartorial and elegant, Serge surrounded himself with beautiful things and beautiful people. And now, after years of being a bachelor, he was looking for a beautiful wife. Karen was determined it would be Anya. Not only did she think they'd get on, but Anya finding a soulmate would let Karen off the hook and allow her to finally walk away.

Anya and Serge's subsequent romance had been intense and its success, Karen liked to think, was down to her own careful management. She'd banned Anya from sending her usual gushy texts and advised her on strategy, making it her business to find out everything about Serge Treblinsky and what made him tick.

And so, when Serge had finally proposed, Karen considered it to be one of her finer achievements. It was a pity she wouldn't actually be able to put it on her résumé.

Anya stopped by the terrace doors and turned.

'What are you wearing tonight, KK?' she asked.

'I hadn't thought.'

'Wear that green dress of mine you like,' Anya said, with a pretty smile.

'Are you sure?' Karen had thought Anya was in one of her moods, but as usual, she was confounded. The offer was incredibly sweet. Anya knew Karen loved that dress.

Anya slipped her shades down her nose and looked mischievously at Karen over the top, with her almond eyes dancing. 'Massimo's coming,' she teased. 'You'll want to look your best.'

Karen blushed. She hadn't dared hope that Massimo would make it to the party. She didn't even know that he was in France.

It had been Serge who had introduced Massimo to Karen at a lunch he'd thrown at his London mansion a few months ago. Serge liked to collect what he called 'real' people, as if Anya's circle of friends was totally fake – an observation Karen considered to be quite correct.

But Massimo was different. He was an artist from Paris, with a gaunt look and the pale hungry eyes of a wolf. He had an unforgettable Gauloises-and-claret-infused husky voice, and seemed to live his life like he was in an art-house film.

Karen wondered now whether Anya and Serge were secretly matchmaking and she felt momentarily wrong-footed. Anya had never suggested that Karen should have any kind of relationship before. Every time Karen had been attracted to someone, Anya had found a way to sabotage it, changing her plans at the last moment so that Karen couldn't make her dates. After a while, she'd stopped bothering to look.

Could it be possible that Anya knew about the conversation that Karen and Massimo had had in the kitchen that night in London? Karen watched Anya giggling and skipping off away from her, as if she'd gleaned some sort of answer.

That conversation. So brief and yet so powerful. Karen remembered every word.

She'd been in the kitchen at the sink, washing a glass, when Massimo had crept up behind her.

'You don't realize, do you?' he'd said.

'What?' she'd asked, feeling her stomach flutter at the sound of his velvety voice.

'You . . . you're so . . .'

'So . . . ?' she'd asked, turning.

'Original.' He'd smiled. 'Exceptional, in fact. It's the most rare thing in the world.'

Karen had gasped, almost dropping the glass. It had been so long since anyone had paid her a compliment.

He'd leant forward, as if sharing a secret. 'I see you, Karen.'

She remembered now the way he'd said her name. As if he were already undressing her. The way his closeness had set butterflies flitting through her stomach. 'I see what you do for Anya. How you are. What you've sacrificed for her. But I see you too. And that is where your true beauty lies.'

But then Anya had walked in, interrupting them, and Massimo had stepped away.

But, Karen decided, shaking the memory from her head, Massimo was the type of man who could trap any woman with his silver tongue. The 'exceptional' thing – that was probably his standard chat-up line. She imagined that he'd had hundreds of lovers. He'd even admitted over dinner that the vintage Mercedes he drove had been a present from an old muse of his – a famous French actress who had taught him everything he knew. How could Massimo ever find an inexperienced person like Karen attractive? Let alone exceptional. He'd probably just been drunk. He probably didn't even remember her name.

Karen was still thinking about the sexy Frenchman as she drove into town later that afternoon to photocopy the lawyers' documents that Anya had signed at lunch. Karen knew that Anya hadn't bothered to read them and needed to make extra copies. She just had time to get to town whilst everyone was taking a siesta. She'd be back to get things ready before anyone noticed she'd gone, or before Serge arrived from the airport with the Pink.

She tuned in the car radio as she sped down the driveway of the Manoir, opening the window and relishing the blast of hot pine-scented air. But as she did so, one of the papers on the passenger seat caught in the draft, and before she could grab it the wind had snatched it away and whipped it out through the open window.

Karen slammed on the brakes and got out, cursing, scrambling behind the bougainvillea to retrieve the paper. Which is when she saw the old Mercedes, partially camouflaged by the trees on the path leading to the summer house.

In the distance, the sun glinted on the sea. Could the car be Massimo's? Had he come to the Manoir early, then broken down on the way to the house?

A wild thought overtook her, causing an unbidden shiver of desire to race to her loins as she walked quickly through the trees.

Maybe he was painting. Maybe she would find him here alone. Maybe . . . something might happen here between them today.

Her heart thumped as she approached the ancient wooden summer house at the edge of the cliffs. It was surrounded by yew trees, some leaning at perilous angles over the cliff edge.

Karen thought about calling out, but instead she slowed, tiptoeing along the path to the side of the house. She wanted to see him before he saw her, to discover if her feelings for him were real, or just something her memory had made up.

There was only one window and through it she had a direct view, all the way from the summer house to the porch.

But instead of finding Massimo alone, painting the amazing view as she'd imagined, what she saw was Anya's naked back pressed up against the glass doors. In front of her Massimo held her, thrusting into her, his eyes half-closed, his mouth pressed against her neck.

Karen jerked back, flattening herself against the wooden boards of the house. She clasped her hands, pressing her fists against her chest, her eyes squeezing shut, as adrenalin rushed through her. It couldn't be . . .

She turned back to take one further look. Still entwined, Massimo had turned Anya around so that Karen could see both their faces. They were staring into one another's eyes, smiling, and as they kissed, it told Karen everything. This was more than just physical infidelity, more than sex. This was what Karen had dreamt of herself, but now saw she could never have.

* * *

She stumbled away, racing to the car and into the town, where she pulled up outside a scruffy roadside bar and downed a brandy to steady her nerves.

How long had they been lovers? Since that lunch in London? For all she knew, Massimo could have been here all summer. How could Karen not have noticed? She'd been so stupid . . . thinking she knew Anya. Thinking she'd secured Anya a good husband and a happy future. Thinking that Anya had finally started to grow up when in reality she'd just kept on being that spoilt little girl who took exactly what she wanted. No matter who she hurt along the way.

So where did that leave poor Serge? Karen had thought Anya loved him. But maybe the truth was that the only thing Anya loved about Serge was his pink diamond.

Because Anya wasn't capable of real love, Karen realized. As far as Anya was concerned, Karen had only ever been a glorified maid. Karen was sure of that now. When had Anya stopped caring? Stopped trusting her? Why had she teased Karen about Massimo this morning, when she was his lover? How could she be so cruel?

Back at the house, Karen threw herself into a frenzy of organization to distract herself until the guests started to arrive. Only then did she summon up the courage to go through the kitchens and up the back stairs to the master suite. She knew she had to confront Anya. She had to stop her from making a mistake. If she didn't love Serge, then she shouldn't marry him. It wasn't fair. Serge was decent and kind. Karen couldn't live with it on her conscience. This deceit. This selfishness. Anya had to be stopped.

Anya's bedroom door was unlocked. Steeling herself, Karen walked inside. The room was vast, with large bay windows overlooking the terrace which was entirely lit with fairy lights. In the distance was the sea, mauve and silver in the evening light. The sound of the jazz band wafted in through the open window.

Then she saw it. On the thick silk bed cushion, with its beautiful pattern of Chinese lilies, a small black box lay open.

The Pink.

For a moment, Karen forgot everything. Without thinking, with her eyes never leaving the diamond, she sat down on the bed, her weight sinking silently into the soft feather mattress.

Mesmerized, she took the box and held the ring up to her face. As close as this, it was even more stunning, its surfaces cut so perfectly that the light bounced and reflected all over the walls and ceiling. The subtle and infinite shades of pink made the diamond seem alive, as if it had a pulsing heart.

Without thinking, she found herself pulling gently at the ring so that the black material around it yielded and it was free. She slipped it on to her ring finger, feeling the almighty weight, yet delicacy of the astonishing ring.

'What do you think you're doing?'

Karen jumped to her feet, the ring box clattering to the floor. Serge stood in the doorway. Karen felt her face burning, guilt resounded through her, piercing as a burglar alarm.

She wished she could disappear, wished she could erase the last minute – the last day of her life, wished she'd never walked in here. And wished, more than anything that Serge wasn't glowering at her from the shadows.

'It was just . . . it's so . . . so . . . beautiful. I couldn't help myself,' she stuttered.

She was terrified that Serge, usually so gentlemanly and placid was about to strike her, or shout, call for Anya. His eyes were so dark, so full of fury.

But suddenly his face relaxed. He walked towards her and smiled, with pity almost, and gently lifted her hands into his and pulled the ring from her shaking finger. 'You are not the first woman to be enthralled by this ring, Karen.'

'Oh Serge, I'm so, so sorry.'

Serge leant down and picked up the box from the floor and replaced the ring. 'But this ring is meant only for one woman,' he continued, ignoring her apologies. 'It can only be worn by a faithful and honest woman, like my mother was with my father.'

Now Karen's own shame gave way to something else – her guilt at knowing Anya's secret.

'Honesty is most important to me, Karen.'

'I wasn't . . .'

Serge held up his hand. 'And the trust of friends.'

Karen stared at him through her brimming eyes. What did he mean? Was he talking about her? Did he think she'd been planning to steal it?

'Like, for example, Massimo,' he continued.

'Massimo?' Karen whispered. What did he know about Massimo?

'He told me just now that he arrived an hour ago.' Serge's gaze was now locked on her like a target. The fury was rising again in his eyes. 'Why do you think he'd lie to me, Karen? After everything I've done for him?'

Karen ripped her eyes away and stared at the carpet, her heart pounding. She stood, penitent, weak with guilt. She should tell him, tell him the truth . . . everything she'd seen in the summer house. But there it was again. Her weakness. Her stupid loyalty to Anya. All the years they'd spent together closed in, like bricks of an impenetrable wall. She couldn't betray Anya. Not tonight. Not without confronting her first. Not without giving her a chance to explain.

Instead, she fought for a lie to tell Serge, but the silence was as solid as a diamond. And just as clear.

'I should go downstairs,' Serge said. 'I don't want to be here when Anya sees the ring. I know how much it means to her.'

He walked to the door. He didn't look back. He pulled the door shut behind him, with an intent and finality Karen didn't understand. She was left there, sealed inside the vacuum of her mistress's room. Just her and the ring. It winked in the soft lighting.

Back downstairs, the party was in full swing. Karen should have felt triumphant, sharing in the buzz of anticipation. Everyone was talking about the Pink and watching the marble staircase down which Anya and Serge were expected any second.

But Karen could only think that the pink diamond was evil. That it had ruined everything.

She looked up as the band stopped. There was an expectant surge in the guests as Serge and Anya appeared through the drawing-room doors at the top of the steps. But then the crowd seemed to recoil as Serge ran down briskly, Anya behind him. He looked serious and stern.

Karen pushed forward through the crowd.

'It's gone,' Serge said, his voice grave. 'The Pink

has been taken. I'm afraid I've had to call the police.'

Suddenly, Anya stormed towards Karen.

'You! You took it!' she shouted, pointing her finger. An ugly flush had risen in her cheeks.

'Anya!' Karen said, shaken. 'No!'

'You were the last person in the room. Where is it? Where is it?' Anya flew at her. 'It's *my* pink diamond. Serge gave it to *me*. Give it back. Give it back!'

Suddenly, Serge was by Anya's side. 'Come on, darling, making accusations isn't going to help.'

'Anya, you're not thinking straight,' Karen said, horrified. 'Of course I didn't take the ring.'

'But you tried it on.'

Karen sensed the crowd moving away from her and heard the ripple of shocked gasps. Serge looked away from her.

'I hate you,' Anya spat at her. 'You've always wanted everything I've got. You've always been jealous. And now you've stolen the most important thing of all.'

Karen had wanted to defend herself, to tell them all the truth about Anya. But from the looks on everyone's faces, she saw that none of them would have listened. She was just staff. A nobody. Her opinion about her hostess didn't matter. They were all on Anya's side. In their eyes she was already guilty.

Karen's sense of indignant humiliation only got worse as the police questioned her, searching her room and belongings. But the Pink remained elusive and as dawn broke, they had no choice but to let her go.

Anya refused to speak to her. She made the lawyer fire Karen with barely a month's pay, insisting that all the gifts she'd given Karen were returned.

And so it was that Karen found herself with a

holdall in the midday heat at the village bus stop waiting for the bus to Nice.

Now, more than anything, she wished that she had taken the ring. But she hadn't been any more capable of doing that than betraying Anya to Serge. Like a beaten dog, she'd been faithful to the end. But it gave her no satisfaction. Any moral high ground that should have been hers had long since vanished. All she was left with was the feeling that she'd been all used up and thrown away.

The hiss of car tyres snagged her attention. A black 4x4 pulled to a stop on the road. The tinted window slid down and Karen recoiled as she saw Serge lean over the seat towards her.

'Get in,' he said. 'I'll give you a lift to the station.'

Karen sat in the passenger seat, wondering when there would be an end to her humiliation. They drove in silence. Karen felt tears stinging her eyes.

'It's not how you think,' Serge said eventually, as if reading her mind. 'Do you remember what I told you? About the ring going to someone faithful and honest?'

'Yes.'

'It will . . .' he paused. 'When she comes along.'

Karen gasped and turned on him, as the implication of what he was saying sank in. 'You mean . . . you . . . ? But I thought the pink diamond was lost?'

'It is. For now. But it will turn up again.'

Karen felt a wave of rage like never before. 'But . . . you? You let her do that to me? In front of all those people.'

'I was being kind.'

'*Kind?*'

'You deserve to live *your* life, Karen. Not Anya's. You should have left long ago.'

Karen couldn't believe what she was hearing. *He'd* done this to her. He'd willingly shamed her. Cost her her job. Ruined her life. How dare he!

Serge smiled. 'Don't be angry. Everything will turn out right. I will see to that.' He gunned the car's engine. 'Your future is an open road. Just like this. It's something you should be excited by, no?'

Karen shook her head, closing her eyes for a second. And the image of the pink diamond suddenly flashed across her mind. The way it had winked in the light.

'Stop the car!' she shouted.

Serge slowed down.

'Stop, I said!'

Karen got out and slammed the door as hard as she could. Serge and Anya . . . she would never understand people like them. They deserved one another.

But now, at last, she was free.

Out of Touch

Carmen
Reid

© Martin Hunter

CARMEN REID is the author of the bestselling novels *Three in a Bed*, *Did The Earth Move?*, *How Was It For You?*, *Up All Night* and *The Personal Shopper*. After working as a journalist in London, Carmen moved to Glasgow, Scotland where she looks after one husband, two children, a puppy, three goldfish and writes almost all the rest of the time. Her new novel, *Late Night Shopping*, is now available from Corgi Books. Visit her website at www.carmenreid.com

Hannah banged the receiver back on to the phone with feeling, then she tried to put the base down but there wasn't any room. There wasn't even one square centimetre of space left, making her wonder where she'd picked the phone up from in the first place.

Her desk was a scene of carnage – no other word for it. The entire eight-foot long by four-feet wide workspace, made by installing a sheet of thick plywood over two second-hand trestles, was completely, utterly and unyieldingly full.

In the centre, marooned like an island in an ocean of clutter, was Hannah's trusty computer. It was old, made of grey plastic and as solid as it was reliable. It still whirred with a noisy electric fan when it sent out an email or saved a file. It didn't make any of those plinky, rinky-dink noises or plip-plop friendly little electric bleeps like her friend Debbie's gleaming new machine.

But Hannah liked it this way. She was an illustrator, she worked from home and this whirring, buzzing, wheezing, asthmatic and slightly arthritic old desktop was her mate. It did everything she needed it to do, very slowly, admittedly. But she didn't need Bluetooth or VoIP ethernet. What the hell was VoIP ethernet anyway?

The heavy, black retro dial phone was still in her hands because she'd not yet been able to reclaim any space on the desk to put it back down. There was something everywhere. Everywhere there was something. From the five flower pots on the right, filled with her work tools: pens, pencils, chewed-up paintbrushes, paint sticks and glue, to the paperwork on the left, stuffed untidily into box files, overflowing in a jumble of white pages with tiny black small print.

But what took up the most space on Hannah's desk were her 'treasures', her supposed 'inspirations'. These were the things she used, or had used, or was maybe planning to use, or would most likely probably never use, but she liked the thought of using them anyway.

There was an array of family photos of course: Doug and their twin girls in all sorts of outfits and expressions. Then several layers of family flotsam and jetsam: a small dolly with a missing arm, a few over-sized liquorice Allsorts made out of clay, a broken window lock, many pencil sharpeners, combs, two pairs of sunglasses, a calculator in sweetie colours, drift-wood, a ball of elastic bands, one or two towering piles of books, many, many postcards, her drawings, draw-ings by the children, art catalogues, yesterday's mail which hadn't yet been processed, broken story tapes, a rubber in the shape of a £20 note, a silver yo-yo.

Hannah had only the vaguest idea as to how all these things had ended up on her desk. Most had landed there unintentionally but once they were there, things tended to stay, in case they became useful somehow in the future. In case she needed them for something. Was it inspir-ation? Or was it constipation? She sometimes wondered.

She pushed back a small pile of books to make some room for the phone, but this set off a landslide of post-cards which had to be headed off by a lightning rearrangement of one of the flower pots. You had to have excellent reflexes to work here.

Perilously close to the edge of the desk, Hannah gingerly set down the phone, hoping this wouldn't cause too much further trouble.

Why did Debbie always do this to her? Hannah acknowledged the clammy feelings of anxiety in the pit of her stomach.

Why did Debbie always dabble? Dabbling Debs. She couldn't leave things alone, could she? She was always stirring, always causing ripples of one sort or another.

Hannah had known Debs since college . . . art college, obviously. Debbie was now a graphic designer who worked in a snazzy loft-style office in town, where she designed packaging – cereal boxes, shoe polish bottles and so on. Although Debs would never say that, she would give her job all sorts of corporate-speak names: 'brand realignment' or 'commodity repositioning'.

Debs actually got whizzy trips to New York to study other people's shampoo bottles and chewing-gum wrappers.

Well, OK, this was sounding bitter. Debs was a talented graphic designer, plus she was your classic extrovert, networky kind of gal. She did well.

Hannah illustrated children's books, which was a sort of Victorian profession in comparison to Debbie's. Hannah hunched over her desk for long hours. She used pens and paints and ink and she slaved and worked and worried.

During the phone conversation which had just ended, Debs had talked about her work, her office, her forthcoming trip to some packaging expo in Chicago, but really the nub of Debbie's call, the nugget of killer gossip offered as soon as the niceties were over, was that she had *bumped into Naz*.

'Can you believe it?' Debs had gushed breathlessly down the line. Naz had also been at college with them. They'd all once been really good friends.

And Debbie just couldn't wait to impart the news that Naz was moving back to Manchester. 'Isn't that just amazing? It's so fantastic!' she had shrieked excitedly.

But Hannah just felt confused. Why was it amazing? Or fantastic? She and Naz had lost touch exactly twelve years ago. Why would they suddenly want to reconnect now? If there had been no reason for her to get in touch with Naz for twelve whole years, if Naz hadn't been invited to her wedding, hadn't even been on the email round robin announcement of the twins being born, why would Hannah want to see him now? Just because he'd moved to Manchester? Just because of some geographical accident?

He hadn't even tried to get in touch with Debbie, he'd just run into her on the street.

But Debbie had told him all about Hannah and what Hannah was doing now. Then Naz and Debbie talking about Hannah had inevitably led to talk about Jake.

Jake had also been at college with them. As soon as he had left, he'd been accepted onto a drama course in London. Then he'd scored a part in a small TV series which had become a major hit and Jake's was now the kind of face nearly everyone in Britain vaguely recognized. He was often photographed attending award ceremonies with a beautiful actress on his arm; he gave interviews about directors it had been 'a privilege' to work with and all that sort of carry on.

Very awkwardly, Jake was also the first person Hannah had been deeply, deeply in love with. And the first person who had loved her very intensely back.

Well, no, that wasn't the awkward thing. Most people fall in love a few times before they find The One and settle down. Lots of people fall in love all over again afterwards as well.

No, it wasn't the having-been-in-love bit that was awkward. What was awkward was their brutal break-up and then the complete, icy silence afterwards.

After four years together, Hannah had left Jake. As she'd never broken up with anyone before, she'd had no idea what to do or what to expect. So she'd done a break-up by numbers. Because she'd still loved Jake very much, even if the 'in love' feeling had worn off, she'd wanted to do the break-up the right way. So she'd done all the things she'd thought you were supposed to do.

She'd told him bravely, tearfully, face to face. She'd left his flat that night with her overnight bag stuffed with all her belongings. Then she didn't contact him again. When he phoned, she didn't answer. When he wrote, she didn't reply. She thought this was what you were supposed to do, to make it easier on both of you. She thought you were supposed to rip the plaster right off.

Just like giving up smoking, she'd gone cold turkey on Jake. And it hadn't been easy. No, at times, it had been hell.

Looking back, which she did only very occasionally now, she wasn't sure that she had done it the right way, even though she'd meant to. She should have checked on him once in a while. She should have phoned up every now and then and made sure he was OK. She should have kept vaguely in touch and not let this great silent gulf open up between them.

Now twelve whole years had passed and the person

she had once loved more than anyone else in the world was still keeping his part of the silence.

Of course she'd thought many times over the years about writing or getting in touch with him again somehow. But now that his face was famous . . . now that he was on television, it seemed creepy, stalkerish even. He must get fan mail and she didn't want to be one of those letters. Imagine getting a reply from his personal assistant or something hideous like that! 'Jake would like to thank you for taking the time to drop him a line. He can't reply personally but . . .'

Urgh! She shuddered at the thought of it.

So she'd let all thoughts of contacting Jake again pass. But now Debbie, dabbling Debbie, Debbie the dabbler had intervened.

'Naz gave me *his* email address,' Debbie had told her, '*Jake's* email address. His very own private one. C'mon!' she insisted, 'get out a pen and write it down!'

With her heart beating fast and her hands shaking slightly, Hannah had obeyed. And now the horrible little scrap of paper, torn from an envelope, was glaring at her . . . daring her.

'Naz said you should drop Jake a line,' Debbie had insisted.

'Jake told Naz he wanted to hear from me?' Hannah had heard herself asking. She was a professional, grown-up, married mother of two, but even she could hear a tinge of pathetic teenage pleading in that question.

'Look, Naz told me to tell you to email Jake, that's all I know,' Debbie had replied.

For several long minutes, Hannah turned the scrap of paper over and over in her hands. She read the letters again and again until she had committed them to memory: 8jakie@aolbox.com.

Oh . . . what the hell, she told herself and rummaged for her computer's mouse under one of the lesser piles of clutter on her desk.

Clicking through to her inbox, she fired up a new message and then saw the big, blank white screen blinking expectantly back at her.

Hi she typed.

No. No, not 'hi'. She deleted that immediately and wrote *Dear* instead.

No. No, she didn't like 'dear' either. She deleted it and re-typed *Hi*. Oh for God's sake, at this pace she was going to be here all day, just squeezing out one paragraph.

Hi Jake,

I got your email address from Naz. Finally, I can drop you a line. How are you? Well, that's almost a silly question, I already know. You're incredibly well and successful and as handsome as ever and I'm so pleased that everything is going so well for you.

Hannah reviewed her work. Good, that was good, it was going well so far. She would bash on, while she was on a roll.

I'm still in Manchester. I got married three years ago to a very nice man called Doug, just before my girls arrived, Jojo and Jessie. Twins!

Oh no! She was one of those women now, detailing her life in terms of who she'd married and who she'd given birth to. Look at that, it was like those pathetic little summaries in the back of her old school magazine.

Totally shocking!! The double exclamation mark made her sound just slightly fun still, didn't it?

I'm an illustrator, which is great. What I always wanted to do, after all. It's tragically underpaid compared with being on TV, as you can imagine! But I can't complain.

Yes, this was going OK. This was upbeat, casual, non-committal, exactly the kind of email she wanted to send.

If you're ever up this way, it would be great to see you. We could have a coffee in the Gramercy bar for old time's sake. It's still there. Hope you're really well, Jake, Hannah xx

Should she say 'love Hannah'? Should she put in her surname? In case he didn't know who it was from? No, surely her name plus Naz and the Gramercy would give him all the clues he needed.

She read the note again and instantly hated it. No. It was just so casual and flippant. It was like one of those pen pal letters you used to write in French class: 'I am thirteen years old and my hobbies include . . .'

She hadn't spoken or written to Jake for *twelve years* – surely she owed him just slightly more than this. Didn't she need to make some sort of apology, some sort of amends?

One moment later and everything that she'd written so far was deleted. She began afresh, taking her time, trying to make some sense of the jumble of emotions running through her mind.

Just the name Jake was enough to bring a host of memories swarming in to her head. Jake wafting about Manchester in the white linen trousers and brocade waistcoats he'd been so into at the time. Jake holding forth in art galleries, Jake's incredibly deep tan which hardly faded at all in the winter, Jake's broad, broad smile and long eyelashes. She could still picture his hands and his voice, she would have been able to recall them even if she hadn't been reminded of them on the television once in a while.

It would be a lie to say that she didn't miss him. He'd been endlessly interesting to know and to love. But friends? She suspected that being friends wasn't going to be easy.

Dear Jake . . . she began afresh:

I don't know where to start. I've finally got an email address for you! I can't tell you how many times I've wanted to get in touch . . . so many. I think if you'd been an ordinary civilian it would have been so much easier. But you of course have to go off and be famous.

Funnily enough, I always thought you would be . . . you're very special, Jake. Still very special to me as well.

I am still, twelve whole years later, so, so sorry about how it ended with us. I know you must have thought it was easy for me, being the person who ended it, but there were so many times afterwards, for such a long time, when I still wasn't sure if I'd made the right decision.

What can I say? I have a wonderful husband and two amazing children . . . but sometimes I still miss you. The way you might miss your best friend from school. Because that's who you were – my best friend . . . for years.

This time Hannah began deleting before she even finished. She was going to have to try again, try and find somewhere between too casual and too heavy.

It was some time before she struck up a third attempt on another bright white screen.

Dear Jake,
I finally have an email address for you. I know it was

a long, long time ago, but it still feels quite nerve-wracking to write to you. OK, well, here I am getting in touch. I know you might not want this, might want to reject it, but never mind. I can live with that, I'm a big girl now. I even have my own babies! Two! Twin girls: Jojo and Jessie.

Anyway, I am so pleased for you, everything looks as if it is working out so wonderfully for you and I'm very happy about that.

Do you ever think about meeting up with me again? I know I would love to. Here's my fantasy version of it: we meet in the Gramercy, because it's still there and I'll definitely need a glass of wine or two to get through it – I mean you're famous now!

I'll bring along my photos (yes, including the totally incriminating ones which you should be very glad I have not yet sold to the Sun!). We'll look through them and have an absolute laugh about the many happy times we had together. And obviously I'll show you my baby and wedding pics and you'll show me the photos of your lovely girlfriend.

And then, that's it, it will be done, my friend. I don't have to worry about bumping awkwardly into you some day when I'm rain-soaked and harassed and wearing the outfit I'd meant to donate to Oxfam.

I hope you're really well, all my very, very best,
Hannah xx

When she'd read it through three times, Hannah felt satisfied. Yes, this was The One. She carefully typed in Jake's email address and then looked it over just one more time.

But now she was no longer so happy . . . now she was

picking holes in all sorts of little things. She hadn't mentioned Doug, she should have mentioned Doug. Where should she put Doug in?

This was getting ridiculous. An entire morning had gone. Her childminder Cathy would be back with the girls any moment now and she still hadn't done a stroke of work.

Damn Debbie, this was all her fault! Why was Hannah still letting herself agonize over this? Just write the bloody note and send it. Or forget about it.

Banging her coffee mug down ferociously, Hannah deleted the message once again. Then she hammered out angry words, not to send, just to vent some frustration.

Jake! Twelve flipping years have gone past. Surely we can just get over it and email each other now and then? Or are you embarrassed to have had such a plain Jane girlfriend once? Someone who's now married with babies? Someone who once dumped screen legend you. Oh let's face it, you always thought you were better than me. If we met up now, you'd no doubt want to remind me of that. You and your rampaging ego. When you were nice, it was like having the star in the centre of the room blaze right at me. When you weren't, you were horrid.

As if a switch had been flicked, suddenly Hannah could only think of bad Jake memories instead of good ones: of waiting and waiting for the phone to ring, of hanging about for hours for him to turn up, of his volatile bad moods and his vicious bouts of unhappiness, of the way he used to almost totally ignore her at parties, making her feel like the least interesting person in the room.

The pointlessness of getting back in touch with him

finally struck her. They both knew exactly how it had been. The good and the bad. What use would there be in meeting for an hour or two at the Gramercy bar and raking over coals which were long burned out? Maybe it was like a fire which had burned very brightly and there just wasn't anything to be rescued from the ashes.

Leaning back in her chair, Hannah reached for her mug, intending to down a mouthful of the cold coffee she knew was lurking at the bottom. As she lifted it from the table, the three postcards which were now propped against it fell sideways, causing a pair of sunglasses balanced precariously on top of four novels, a diary and an old travel guide to Italy to slide off. This set an avalanche, a bunfight of agendas, notebooks, stiff paintbrushes, rulers, pencils, hairclips and biros into motion. They were off! They were falling and slipping in every direction.

As Hannah made a grab for a notebook, she brushed against her faithful old red Filofax. The heavy leather one she'd had for at least ten years now, all cracked and faded. The Filofax, unbalanced, slid down and thunked on top of her mouse.

With a feeling of panic so intense it made her feel sick, she heard the dull whirring start up and to the sound of Hannah uttering an impassioned 'Noooooooooooo!' the rude and ranting email whirred off into cyberspace, to pitch up completely unintentionally at Jake's address.

Hannah was in a place beyond horror: nothing for twelve years and now she'd sent some completely unprovoked rant into his inbox unannounced.

Nooooooooo!

She stared at the screen, open-mouthed with

disbelief and shock. What could she do? Could she send some sort of disclaimer? 'Hi Jake, you weren't supposed to get this . . . it was for someone else . . . a mad person wrote this on my computer and sent it for a joke . . .' Debbie! Could Debbie somehow take the blame?

But Hannah's head crumpled down on to the pile of chaos on her desk. That wasn't going to do. That was impossible, stupid, would just make her look even worse, even more ridiculous.

Oh, how could this have happened?

Then she heard the whirr again, the little buzz of the motor starting up into life. Did she have new mail? She couldn't bear it. She couldn't look, she couldn't even open her eyes. This was horrible!

Could it really be a reply from him? After all this time out of touch, could he really have emailed her back within a minute? No. It wasn't likely, was it? Jake was hardly going to be sitting at his computer twiddling his thumbs. Anyway, he would never reply to the thing that she'd just sent, would he?

Still, she prised her head up from the side of the desk, unscrewed her eyes just enough to be able to make out the name of the sender: dbe.apple@ gwizzgraphics.com

It was Debbie. Dabbling Debbie who'd got her into this horrible, cringe-making mess in the first place.

Debbie, you terrible twit! Hannah shouted out loud at the screen.

Reluctantly, she dragged her mouse out from under the Filofax, postcards and associated scrum, and clicked on the message.

In front of her eyes were saviour words which she was

so astonished to see, she had to read them several times over.

'Sorry, Hannah, gave you wrong email for Jake. It's 8jakie@aolinbox.com. Might not make a difference, but just in case.'

Hannah allowed herself to breathe a sigh of slight relief. It had to make a difference. In cyberspace these tiny little details were important! Hadn't Doug told her this at length when he was installing her new software?

As she watched the screen and waited for the proof that she'd got the address wrong to arrive, she knew now what a huge mistake it was to even think about getting back in touch with Jake again.

They had both recovered completely from their injuries; the scars were all well and truly healed. What good could possibly come of revisiting the scene of the crime?

She should not have even thought of it for a moment.

The growl from the depths of the computer's engine started up again . . . something was coming in. With every finger crossed, Hannah looked up at the latest inbox arrival.

Never, ever had the words 'Mail delivery failure' looked so good.

Weak with relief, she swept a deliberate arm slowly across a corner of her desk, sending a great heap of books, papers, bits, pieces and junk all flying to the floor.

The past was . . . past. But right here, right now, she had some serious tidying up to do.

The Party

Susan Sallis

SUSAN SALLIS was brought up in Gloucestershire and now lives with her family in Clevedon, Somerset. She is the author of over twenty bestselling novels and her latest, *Rachel's Secret*, will be published by Corgi Books in October.

A thirtieth birthday is a definite watershed. Twenty-nine is still bearable until the end of it is about a month away. If mistakes are made they are excused by older people . . . 'She's still in her twenties . . . she'll learn.' At thirty and then thirty-something, things are expected of you. It's no longer a rather nice surprise when you cope with a dinner for six at a four-place table. It's rather a shame in fact that you still have a four-place table. By thirty you should have accomplished something besides inner peace. Something tangible if materialistic. A six- or even eight-place table would be nice for starters.

It was Rob who thought up the Family Party. Whether he imagined that would be less of a strain than Dinner with Friends, I'm not sure. But he got enthusiastic.

'It might kill two birds with one stone,' he said, narrowing his eyes as if he was working out one of his maths problems. 'We could cut down on the Christmas visits perhaps. Anyway, we don't have to make enormous efforts for family. A buffet, sausage rolls and sandwiches. Intimate, yet encouraging both sets of relatives to mingle.'

He had no idea. His parents and my mother got on well. But what about my uncle Cecil who remarried last year for the third time? Rob's cousin, Roland, regularly referred to him as The Old Goat. And sausage rolls and sandwiches? It's my thirtieth for goodness' sake; things are expected of me.

I said weakly, 'We still have to lay out the food. Have somewhere to put it.'

Rob's eyes narrowed to slits. 'That enormous old door shoring up the compost. When we bought the house Mr Chapman told me it had come from the Manor. Mahogany, he said.' He opened his eyes wide; they were blue, very blue. He smiled. 'We can scrub it up and lay it over our table!'

I thought of all the gunge that would have to be scrubbed; even so I murmured, 'Savouries down one side, puddings the other. An orderly line of people. Can't you just hear your aunts and Cousin Roland . . .' I put on a mincing voice intended to be an amalgam of Rob's relatives. ' "Onion bhajis. Splendid." "Don't you just love spring rolls?" "Oh my God, a roulade – hold me back, someone."'

Rob knew I was won over and he could afford to dampen me slightly. He said austerely, 'Those three items are heartily disliked by my aunts, Cousin Roland and his stick-thin wife respectively.'

'Well, I know foreign food is a bit controversial with the oldies, but surely Roland and Marguerita will enjoy it? And just about everyone else will go mad for roulade. I'll get two or three from Langley's Patisserie, they do a lemon one that is irresistible.'

'That's true. Jenny and Pete will love them.'

I said nothing. The twins were almost six years old. Rob thought everyone adored them, which they probably did in very finite bits of time. But Jenny loves an audience, and when she is famous Pete will be her agent and promote her just as he has done since birth really. In other words, the two of them tend to take over.

They were excited about my birthday; only last year

they had been mildly surprised that anyone much taller than they were had birthdays. I played down the intimate gathering.

'But it's your *birthday* party,' Jenny protested. 'I can sing.'

'We can do all that at breakfast, darling. And it's not exactly a party.'

'Not just 'Happy Birthday', Mum! I can *sing*!' She searched her repertoire for something suitable. 'I can sing "Don't Fence Me In"!'

My mother had taught her this song, it dated from the Second World War and involved thigh slapping and a hideous American cowboy accent. Pete was ecstatic. 'That's my fave, too,' he confided.

'I'm not really old enough for that particular song.'

Jenny spread her arms and went into a sentimental ballad from the First World War. Pete applauded. Rob was having difficulty stifling his laughter. 'I'm not laughing at you, sweetie,' he told his daughter. 'It's Mum's face!'

Pete sprang to my defence. 'She can't help getting old!' He gave me a strangle-hug. 'I love your face, Mum.'

I gave Rob a look that cut off his laughter at the first guffaw.

I said, 'Good. But you can see that the sort of party you've got in mind is not really me any more.' Dammit, I was starting to believe that. Why hadn't we invited the neighbours with their various broods and gone in for afternoon buns and lemonade in the garden? Jenny could have sung to her heart's content and Derek, Anna, Phyllida and Dominic would have told her in no uncertain terms when they'd had enough.

I added, 'There won't be any other children, darlings.

This is a family party and so far we are the only ones with children. I'm sure that will change,' I added doubtfully thinking of stick-thin Marguerita and my brother's model-type wife, Janice.

'She can sing a couple of songs.' Rob looked at me pleadingly. 'Have tea – they can choose what they like from the buffet – sing to everyone, then bedtime.'

The twins exchanged glances. But we had already worked out that my birthday would fall on a Sunday this year which meant school the next day, so after some unsuccessful wheedling they surrendered.

We had just over three weeks to plan and prepare and as it was a family do and totally informal, Rob assured me that was more than enough time. I pointed out that the garden needed tidying up; Rob was astonished.

'It will be October by then!'

'The clocks don't go back until the very end and even if it's pouring with rain it will be light enough for my sister-in-law to see that absolutely nothing has been done since she was here last!'

Rob got the message; if I am calling Janice my 'sister-in-law', I am getting edgy. Janice makes my brother ecstatically happy. She is beautiful. She is PA to a corporate lawyer. She is great fun. She is twenty-six.

Rob said, 'I'll see to the garden, don't worry. It's your birthday. You shouldn't have to do anything. We'll make lists. It might be as well if you do the food though.' He put his arms around me and started the butterfly kisses along my eyebrows. I felt myself melting. Then he murmured, 'I cannot believe that you are thirty.'

I said ungrammatically, 'Not yet I'm not!'

He removed the comb that kept my hair up and

moved his lips to my right ear. 'People will think you are lying about your age. You still look like you did at nineteen on the People and Environment march, with your hair in your eyes and that damned banner held high!' His laugh whispered right into my head. 'Your mother was so right to call you Pansy – all right, all right, I know you hate the name, but think of those brown and gold flowers, always open to all weathers. Your eyes are that same brown and your hair is . . .'

'Rob, stop it! I know what you're doing and I don't need reassurance about my age! Nothing wrong with being thirty. Just because you've got another six months to go before you get there—'

He was laughing into my hair, nibbling my neck, crowing with schoolboy delight. 'Cradle snatcher!' he spluttered as I wriggled helplessly. 'Casting your older-woman spell over a mere youth, a whole half year younger than you! It's nothing short of—' he couldn't think of a word. He's a scientist and works at the government research station, his vocabulary is therefore limited.

I told him this as I struggled out of our sofa, which had seen much better days before the twins. But then he kissed me properly and stopped laughing and I fell back into the sofa and put my hands behind his head; his hair was brown and thick and curly at the back. There's something about the nape of his neck that causes complete meltdown.

Eventually we made some lists. Invites. Garden. Scrub door and fit it on to present dining table. Clean house. Food. Rob said that written invitations took too long and were too formal for our intimate family gathering;

he would phone. I said I would do my relatives. He said no, I would take half an hour for each one. He would do them all.

He was as good as his word. And they all accepted which was a bit of a blow because eighteen people in our modern semi was a bit much when at least half a dozen of them needed comfortable chairs from which they would be unwilling to move.

'I was absolutely relying on Uncle Cecil and his new wife to be going to their time-share,' I mourned. 'He's so . . . large.'

'But she'll sit on his lap,' Rob comforted. 'She makes a point of sitting on his lap.' We giggled and I pointed out that our armchairs would not take that kind of weight. Rob said tentatively that it could make the party go with a swing. I told him to be serious; there was so much to *do*. He asked where I kept the secateurs and said he'd start on the garden so that if the weather held we could light lanterns and Uncle Cecil and the new wife could be really romantic and sit outside.

He made a good start. Plus, with a week still to go he talked the twins into letting us put the slide and the swing in to the shed for their winter hibernation. The four of us stood by the kitchen door and admired the garden.

'It's bloody enormous,' Jenny commented.

Even Pete stared at her incredulously. Jenny said, 'It's what Daddy said to you last night, Mum. I was hanging my knickers on the drain pipe and I heard him say that the garden looked bl—'

'Hanging your knickers on the drain pipe?' If I had been more shockable I might have fainted. To reach the drain pipe, Jenny would need to open her casement window, stand on a chair and lean right outside. Rob had put childproof bolts on the upstairs casement windows. And anyway, why did her knickers need to be hung on the drain pipe?

Jenny realized she had slipped up big-time. She was very clever. She said, 'Actually, Dominic thinks that "bloody" shouldn't be a swear word anymore because everyone says it all the time. Daddy does. And you do too sometimes, Mum.'

I could tell she was rattled and when Rob said he would put the kettle on and why didn't I sit down while he fixed the window, she began to cry. Pete put an arm around her and glared at us. Usual family stuff of course, but deep down and almost subconsciously, I blamed it on the party and therefore on becoming thirty. I said I wouldn't sit down, I would have a walk around our bloody big garden if no one minded. I left Rob to have the serious chat about never leaning out of an upstairs window. As I fought my way between the rhodies, which would need a lot more work with the secateurs before we could call it a shrubbery, I heard Pete say, 'This boy at school says he was on the train and a man put his head out of the window and it was knocked off on the side of a bridge!' Jenny stopped crying and asked if the man found it. Pete said, 'I don't know. I'll ask the boy. His name is Oliver. I wish you'd called me Oliver, Dad.'

So the garden was almost done, the childproof bolts were checked and found wanting so all the casements were screwed shut permanently and there were three days to go. It was Wednesday and I was chatting with the neighbours at the school gates, the high spot of my day actually. We were going out for a meal in a week's time to celebrate my birthday and Amanda's. Amanda would be thirty-five and did not seem bothered. She told me I'd soon get used to a three instead of a two.

The bell clanged, the children burst forth. Pete was with Oliver, Jenny was with her teacher.

'No, everything's fine,' she said as I surged forward. 'Just a quick word. I wonder whether you can find a way of explaining the difference between hearing and listening.' She grinned. Jenny grinned too. She adored Miss Hutchings and wanted her to marry Mr Hilton who was the PE specialist. Mr Hilton was already married.

We walked home, Pete and Jenny went to Amanda's house. I could hear Pete telling Jenny that Oliver had not actually seen the man beheaded; his aunty had told him about it when he stuck his own head through the train window. Jenny listened to that all right because she immediately denounced Oliver as a liar. Pete defended him hotly. I let myself in to our wonderfully empty, quiet house, opened the patio doors and looked down the big empty garden and thought I would spend an hour cutting back the rhodies, fetch the children from Amanda's, feed them and have them in the bath when Rob arrived home. They love their bath, it's enormous. They call it Bigfoot because it stands on splayed and rusty feet. We ought to change it; it uses too much water and the chipped enamel has been painted over inexpertly by Mr Chapman. But the twins think it's great.

I'd just found the secateurs hanging where they should be, when the phone rang. It was Rob.

'Darling, I don't know what to do. The environmental

conference. In Brussels. They want a representative from Research. They've asked me. It's what we talked about ten years ago, Pan. It's why you walked that banner all along the bloody Mall. But . . . oh God, it's your birthday and it's a big one and I want to be there with you.'

I did not hesitate. 'You have to go, Rob. You know very well. You have to go. There just might be a chance for you to speak. Tell them about the twins. Tell them that all the kids in the whole world deserve clean air and water—'

'Pan. Darling girl. I would be an observer only. Anyone here can do it. I don't know why they've chosen me.'

I was crying. 'They've chosen you because you are the best! You *think*. You think all the time. Rob, you have to do this. I am so proud of you, so very, very proud . . .'

'But your birthday – I would have to fly out tonight and I won't be back until Sunday morning.'

'Then you won't miss a thing, you idiot! I plan to be thirty all day long!'

There was a long pause during which I managed to stop crying. He said quietly, 'I love you, Pan.' Another pause while I sniffled my love to him, then he said, 'Can you pack a case for me? That old yellow grip will be fine. I'll wear my suit, so jeans and T-shirts. Shoes, socks. You know.'

So that's why the rhodies did not have a haircut and that's why after the taxi had taken Rob off to the airport and I had told the over-excited twins just what the conference was all about – and I swear that Jenny listened to every word – and I had tucked them into bed and brought them down to earth with their favourite Tintin story, I was so exhausted I went to bed myself.

* * *

It was Thursday, party day minus two. Took kids to school. Rob rang, nice hotel but he could not remember the colour of the walls in his room. Amanda offered coffee; I just looked at her and she said, 'Sorry.' Cooked. Rob rang, Americans still refusing to be persuaded. Caught sight of myself in hall mirror; flour in hair; damn, another shampoo and there'd been an item on telly about natural oils . . . To show I was listening I said, 'Which one is the nicest nation?' There was an incredulous silence then Rob laughed. 'Very amusing. Nicest nation indeed. Got to go.' Cooked on. Met kids. Miss Hutchinson looked out of the cloakroom door and stuck her thumb up. We ate in the garden to save messing up the house. Spent all evening scrubbing the door which propped up the compost heap. Could still smell it after bath and a gallon of body oil.

Friday came. Rob phoned. Door still smelling of manure. Poured a bottle of bleach over it and took the kids to school. Oliver called across the playground, 'I am *not* a liar! All right?' Amanda said, 'I know how you feel. He's the most popular boy in the school.' I hadn't worried about it until she said that. But with thirty years of life over and done with on Sunday, I was worrying about everything starting with plane crashes and now ending with Jenny being mugged by the whole school. That's what getting old does for you. You turn into your mother and worry about everything.

I went straight through to open up the patio doors and sniff the bleach-soaked door, and there was my mother, my very own mother, sitting on her suitcase and looking at the door smilingly. As if she had been talking to it.

I screamed 'Mum!' at the top of my voice and she screamed 'Pan!' at the top of hers and we clutched each other and rocked and then did a kind of slow foxtrot around the door.

She freed herself and said, 'Why didn't you tell me? Rob rang last night and I packed a case and caught the coach just by where Jenkins' shop used to be first thing this morning – you remember Jenkins' shop – you used to love his barley sugar.'

'Mum, you're supposed to be a *guest* for God's sake! You told me Uncle Cecil and his new wife were picking you up at three o'clock on Sunday afternoon and you were bringing a sherry trifle and two dozen of your butterfly cakes.'

We went on like this for some time. The fact was that my mother had come to rescue me. She played bridge on Fridays and did her shopping in Bath on Saturday mornings. But she was here. She was going to do the cakes and the trifle today and decorate them tomorrow when the children were at home. She looked through my larder then asked me whether I could drive her to the supermarket for a few odds and ends. We had lunch there. Time was going and I just didn't mind. I was thinking in whole sentences again. I told her about Jenny calling Oliver a liar and she laughed her head off.

'He's bitten off more than he can chew there,' she said. 'That child is so like you at the same age.'

I said almost sadly, 'And I'm starting to be like you.'

She took my hand as it lay on the table doing nothing. 'That's how it goes. It's one of the other things that makes the world go round,' she said.

She took all her stuff in to the kitchen and cooked, and I dealt with the smelly door and found some ancient carpets in the attic that would smother the compost heap completely. Between us we placed the good old door on to the four-place table, covered the whole thing with a sheet, and put a pile of plates on top to hold it all down. Rob rang. It was going to be stalemate again but not quite so stale as before. He had hopes. 'Let me talk to Pete and Jen. I need to get them young.'

'Mum's fetching them from school.'

'She's with you? Great. I love your mum, Pan.'

'So you won't mind too much if I turn into her later?'

'Ah.' He thought about it during which time Jenny had arrived, taken the receiver and was telling him that she had asked Oliver to be her boyfriend and he had said all right. Pete found room for his ear and they listened together for some time. Then Pete – not Jenny – said, 'But Dad, we always say 'world without end' so it will go on and on even if we use up the sorts.' He frowned and repeated after his father, 'Sources. Not sorts. Even if we use up everything it will go on without end.' And Jenny said soberly, 'It won't be the same though, will it?'

Mum came in from the hall. She was carrying four plastic-covered pizzas. 'From your friend, Amanda,' she mouthed. 'What a lovely girl. When she saw me, she rushed back into her house and brought out this fourth one.'

We ate them outside and talked about the school's latest can-stamp. The children collected all the drink cans they could and once a week on a Friday they stamped them flat and packed them into plastic containers for the collectors. 'It's called mental institutions,' Pete told his grandmother solemnly. She understood perfectly, 'Environmental issues are very important. That's why your father is very honoured to be attending the conference in Brussels.'

'That's where they grow sprouts,' Jenny told her.

To be honest I had forgotten the reason for the party and was surprised and delighted when breakfast in bed arrived on Sunday morning with a pile of presents surrounding boiled egg and toast. Jenny and Pete had made a photograph frame from a cornflake packet. Old snaps of me as a baby (from Grandma), Rob and me (from Daddy) and all of us in the garden (raided from this summer's collection) were stuck on to the inside back of the box and a sheet of sandwich wrap covered the front. It was beautiful. I hugged them ecstatically.

Mum had given me her mother's garnet necklace. 'You might as well have it while it matches your hair,' she said.

At three thirty the doorbell and telephone rang in unison. Mum went for the door so I picked up the phone. It was Rob. He was still at the airport in Belgium. 'Happy birthday, Pan. I can't bear to be missing it. There's just a chance I'll sleep with you tonight. If that's OK?'

'Oh Rob . . .'

'No, don't – just stop it. Otherwise I'll have to start swimming.' He gulped. 'Seriously Pan. Don't cry. Not on your birthday. You're a big girl now and big girls don't.'

'I won't if you won't.' Hearty sounds came from the hall. 'Oh my God. It's Uncle Cecil and his new wife. Two hours early! Darling, take care. Just take care and be safe. D'you hear me?'

'The whole airport probably hears you, Pan. You should have been here, the conference delegates would have had to listen to you.'

I was already enveloped in Uncle Cecil's hug. The new wife tottered behind him holding a clingfilmed platter of sandwiches. Uncle Cecil said, 'We've brought the gazebo. I'll take it round the side in to the garden. Doesn't take a minute. I'll do the bar in there . . . no problem. Is this a family occasion or what?'

'May dear, how lovely to see you.' Mum greeted the new wife by name and made appreciative sounds as she whipped off the clingfilm and stabbed the sandwiches with small flagstaffs announcing that half were smoked salmon and the other half honey roast ham. She kissed Mum. 'I said to Cecil, this sort of thing is just marvellous, not only to say happy birthday to darling Pansy but to keep in touch with everyone.' She kissed me gratefully and put her hand into Uncle Cecil's inside pocket. I thought they were at it already, but no, she produced a long flat box and they both sang 'Happy Birthday' to me and then insisted on me opening it. A Victorian dress clip studded with garnets exactly matching my grandmother's necklace. I was overcome. My mother gathered the twins to her and said, 'Let's watch Uncle Cecil put up the gazebo and have tea inside it. How about that? You can pour, Jenny, and Pete can pass it around.'

During the next two hours people kept arriving, everyone was early, everyone brought food and presents. Rob's aunts, Esme and Dorcas, brought three Thermos flasks of soup in case the weather turned cold. Roland and Marguerita produced two dozen bags of fat-free crisps. Marguerita was no longer thin; she was expecting a baby by Christmas and was very proud of her high bump and longing to talk to me about labour and relaxation methods. Pete ushered her into the gazebo and said kindly, 'You got to breathe right out, even when you think you have, you really haven't. I can make myself go to sleep like that.'

My brother, Bill, was dancing with Mum; his wife, Janice, was doing the music. She pounced on me and we did a crazy dance around the sofa. Jenny pulled Esme to her feet and I grabbed Dorcas. Outside, Uncle Cecil continued to dispense drinks beneath the gazebo and his new wife was lighting the lanterns and hanging them everywhere. Rob's sister appeared and asked what I'd done with Rob. I told her what had happened and waited for her to marvel at what some people would do to get out of a party. But she said genuinely, 'Oh Pan. What a damned shame! After all the fuss about the garnets too. Pan, this is my fiancé . . . no, well we didn't tell anyone for ages in case it went pear-shaped – neither of us is very good at commitment. We decided we'd tell you and Rob and a few others . . . you know.' He was nice. I said I would tell Rob. I planned privately to warble 'What a difference a man makes.'

There were people I didn't recognize but they were all happy together and as a sort of purple darkness set in around the rhododendrons and Uncle Cecil and his new wife disappeared, I stood behind the bar in the gazebo and tried to remember everything to tell Rob. And then there was a strange squeaking noise from above and suddenly Jenny's window opened and she and Marguerita leaned out. Pete's head bobbed up too. They began to sing 'Happy Birthday'. I brandished a bottle at them which they thought was a request for an encore. Jenny sang 'Don't Fence Me In'. Roland trumpeted to Marguerita to 'come down at once', she had the baby to consider.

It was well past bedtime. The twins came down and let Grandma help them choose a plate of food to eat in bed and I took the screwdriver upstairs and tried to repair the damaged window. Marguerita must be very much stronger than she looked to force that bloody casement open.

Rob must have arrived at the same time as the twins took the last plate from the pile and upset the entire balance of Mr Chapman's door. It sounded as if we were being ram-raided. I fell downstairs as fast as I could and just about registered the total destruction of the buffet before being swept off my feet by Rob and whirled around the room, through the kitchen, out in to the garden, and down the garden where we finally crashed into the shed.

Everyone was cheering, Mum was saying loudly, 'Don't worry, children. We can eat off the floor. Your mother has cleaned it every day since she married your father.' Treating this as forgiveness on the spot, Jenny broke yet again into 'Happy Birthday'. Everyone took it up.

But the shed was yet another of Mr Chapman's Heath Robinson legacies and as we leaned against it, laughing helplessly, it gave a groan and fell to pieces wall by wall. And there, exposed in every sense of the word, were Uncle Cecil and his new wife. The lanterns bobbed beneath the moon and shone on them just in case anyone was missing anything. I think it was Rob who led the applause, though Bill was not far behind.

Actually Mum missed that because she was halfway

up the stairs getting the twins to bed and out of any possible trouble. Everyone else seemed to enjoy it very much indeed and Rob's aunts thought the whole thing had been planned.

'I know Cecil is an extrovert,' Dorcas said to Bill and Janice, 'but even in this modern age, surely this is going rather too far?'

Uncle Cecil thought we should do it again at Christmas. Janice thought that was a great idea and my dear brother, Bill, nodded vigorously.

Eventually they went home and we cleared up and sat talking until it wasn't my birthday any longer and I was already getting used to the plump luscious digit known as three. Rob's present was a pair of garnet earrings exactly matching Grandma's necklace. Bill and Janice had provided the bracelet and Uncle Cecil the dress clip. Yes, as Rob's sister had told me already, there had been a great fuss about matching everything to my eyes and hair.

I have never had a birthday quite like my thirtieth. Perhaps I never will again. But to have it once is quite a privilege. As Jenny said soulfully the next day, 'Reminds me of that old song you taught, Grannie. 'All You Need Is Love'. Shall I sing it now or wait until Oliver calls for me to go to school?'

The Best
Birthday Ever

PATRICIA
SCANLAN

© Peter Orford

PATRICIA SCANLAN was born in Dublin, where she still lives. She is the author of several bestselling novels, the latest, *Forgive and Forget*, will be published by Transworld Ireland in July. Patricia is the series editor and a contributing author to the *Open Door* series. She also teaches Creative Writing to second-level students and is involved in Adult Literacy.

How do you know when a friendship is over . . . kaput . . . past its sell-by date?

I'm sitting in a coffee shop waiting to meet my oldest 'friend' to tell her that her daughter will not be invited to my daughter's forthcoming birthday party and that, in fact, will no longer be part of my daughter's circle of friends.

I take a sip of creamy latte. My stomach feels slightly fluttery as apprehension grips me. Yet I know this moment has been coming for a long time. It was something I should have done many months ago but I'd stubbornly held on to the notion that Alison Cassidy and I had a long, enduring friendship. Who was I kidding? And what did it say about me and my ostrich-like behaviour that I still thought like that?

We were a strange pair, Alison and I. Even as kids the contrast between us was striking. We both lived on the same street, Alison three doors down from me. She, skinny, gangly, driven to succeed; me, short, plumpish, easy-going. Chalk and cheese. As a child I didn't realize that Alison felt superior to me. That came later as I grew up and gained a modicum of self-knowledge. I certainly didn't feel superior to Alison then, but I felt sorry for her. There is a difference. Alison's parents were divorced. Her father left Alison's mother and moved in with a toned, tanned estate agent he'd met at the gym, when Alison was seven, just a little younger than our daughters. It must have been horrific, I think, still able to feel sorry for Alison for all the pain, grief and anxiety she'd endured as a child.

I can remember her little pinched, worried face as she knuckled down to her studies, even then, so that she could get a good job and become very rich so her mom wouldn't have to worry about bills. She was never going to get married, she told me.

Alison was very possessive of our friendship and hated it if I played with the other kids. I was outgoing and friendly and railed against her sulks and tantrums and 'Do you like so-and-so better than me?' interrogations. Now, of course, I can see how completely insecure she was, and how the fear of rejection informed all of her behaviour, right into adult life.

'You have to be kind to Alison,' my mom would insist when I'd moan that I was sick of her and didn't want to play with her any more. 'See how lucky you are. Our family has fun; we have Dad to take care of us and have good times with.'

'Yeah, but she says things about us. She says we're silly 'cos we believe in Santa and go to pantos and that's only for kids.'

'She's only jealous, Claire, take no notice,' my mother said kindly, ignoring my fierce, bubbling resentment and making me feel mean for moaning.

How old patterns repeat themselves. I'd been saying the same sort of thing to my eight-year-old daughter, Joanna, about Alison's daughter, Kristen.

Joanna and Kristen had been 'friends' since they were born, with only six weeks between them. And it was like watching a re-run of my relationship with Alison. Kristen, pushy, driven, combatative, competitive. Joanna, open, laid-back, cheerful, and very soft-hearted.

My heart melted as I thought of my beloved daughter. She was such a good kid and a loyal friend, and Kristen had never valued her, had only nagged and niggled at her, comparing and contrasting her own edgy, unsatisfactory existence with Joanna's happy-go-lucky and very secure environment.

Don't get me wrong. Kristen has a very affluent lifestyle. Alison and her husband Stuart are both well-off, successful lawyers with a thriving practice. They'd met at college and Alison found a soulmate, someone as ambitious and driven and hungry for success as she. They married when they qualified, and set up in business together. Now theirs is the biggest legal practice in town. They have three foreign holidays every year, a villa on a golf resort in the Algarve, flashy cars, a big house and private schooling for Kristen.

Kristen has her own TV and DVD in her bedroom, a computer, Wii, iPod, everything her little heart desires; while my Joanna shares a bedroom with her younger sister, Ella, is allowed computer time and TV time, and goes to the country for six weeks in the summer, to a mobile home.

'I'm so lucky I have my own room and all my own stuff, I can watch what I want and do what I want, that's much better than your stupid "family time",' Kristen had boasted recently. Joanna had been fire-engine red with rage.

'Mom, Kristen said our family time is stupid. She's really rude. I'm sick of her saying things about us all the time.'

'And what do *you* think? Do you think our family time is stupid?' I enquired, used to their squabbling.

'No, I think it's fun,' Joanna declared, her little freckled nose flaring in indignation.

We have a rule in our house that everyone sits down to the family meal together. The TV is turned off, computers put to sleep, and for an hour or two my husband, Frank, and I sit and natter with our kids about their day at school and our day at work.

Kristen had stayed for dinner one day and had been aghast that the TV had been turned off in the middle of *Drake and Josh*.

'I'll eat my dinner on a tray,' she insisted.

'No, you won't. You can sit at the table with us. This is our family time,' I'd explained.

'But I always eat my dinner in front of the TV. My childminder lets me,' she whined.

'Nope, come on, sit with us and eat up,' I'd instructed firmly, watching her cross little face and thinking how like her mother she was at that age. She'd sat sulkily, while the girls and I began to talk about the events of our day as Frank ladled spoonfuls of tasty chicken casserole on to her plate.

In spite of herself she began to eat. She always cleared her plate in our house. Her childminder fed her pizzas and processed meals that could be heated up in a microwave, so a home-cooked meal was a rare treat.

Kristen hadn't made her 'family time is stupid' announcement in my hearing. She knew better. I always took her to task if she stepped over a boundary, much to her annoyance, but I could imagine her superior little puss with her blonde hair tossed back as she made her cutting remark to Joanna. She knew how to push my daughter's buttons, and as they got older their relationship was becoming more fractured and fractious.

'She's only jealous because she doesn't have family

time,' I pointed out to Joanna. 'Her mom and dad are too busy. They don't get home from work until late.'

'Yeah, well she says her mom says you don't have a proper job, you only work for peanuts,' Joanna said crossly.

Smug bitch, I thought, feeling an uncharacteristic flash of fury, and a frisson of hurt. OK, so my mornings-only job-share as an office administrator in a busy primary school might not pay the huge salary Alison was accustomed to but it was certainly more than peanuts and, more importantly for me, it meant I was at home in the afternoon when my daughters finished school and I cooked their dinner and did their homework with them, and not some poorly paid child-minder who didn't give a toss.

I know Alison had made the remark. Kristen wouldn't have come up with it herself and I suppose it was that dismissive observation that made me take a good, long hard look at my 'friendship' with Alison.

I take another sip of latte and glance at my watch. Twelve fifteen. Alison was supposed to be here at twelve. Typical. She's always late when we arrange to meet. She is firmly of the opinion that her time is far more precious than mine. She is, after all, a lawyer. They now live in an exclusive gated estate just outside of town. They go to all the posh dinner parties and hold even posher ones themselves. Needless to say Frank and I never get invited to them. I get invites to meet in coffee shops.

I'd been invited to lunch once or twice in the Taj Mahal, as Frank had christened it, when they'd first moved into it, but the invites had dwindled over the past few years. I can't even remember when I was there last.

No, a coffee shop was deemed suitable for me, not even the chic new wine bar on Abbey Lane that was doing a roaring trade, where Alison might see colleagues or clients and would have to introduce me to them.

It was now twelve twenty-five. I had taken a precious day's leave to visit the dentist and buy Joanna's birthday present and order her cake. I could be having a manicure or a mini facial, or even a tapas lunch, in my favourite haunt, Domingo's Tapas Bar down in the Square. Instead I was twiddling my thumbs, sipping a now cold latte, waiting for someone who didn't value my friendship or my time.

It helped that by the time Alison arrived, I was steaming.

'Sorry I'm late,' she said airily as she dropped her Louis Vuitton briefcase by her skyscraper heels and sat down opposite me. She was wearing a sharply cut black trouser suit with a cream silk cami. Her hair, in a short feathery style was perfectly highlighted. I felt almost dowdy beside her although I had dressed with care in a long straight black skirt, and a short, burgundy, nipped in at the waist jacket that gave me a good shape and drew the eyes away from my ass, which was starting to head south.

'I won't be able to stay too long seeing as I'm running late,' Alison announces as she waves imperiously at a young waitress. I seethe with resentment. *She* delays me by almost half an hour and *she* has the cheek to tell me she's running late.

'That suits me. I'm short on time myself. I didn't think I'd be twiddling my thumbs here for twenty-five minutes,' I say curtly.

'Oh!' She looks at me in surprise. I don't think she's ever heard me use that tone before.

'Sorry. Our conference call ran over. It's a very important case. Very hush-hush but there are planning implications for the town,' she confides.

Her cases were always 'very important', I thought, unimpressed, as the waitress stood poised to take our order. 'Green tea for me and no chocolate on the side,' Alison declares briskly, eschewing the big round chocolate sweet that always accompanied the teas and coffees. I love the taste of melting chocolate and hot coffee.

'Regular coffee for me please.' I smile. I'm certainly not ordering another latte in front of Alison.

'So, great to see you, Claire, what's new? What's hip and happening?' Alison sits back in her chair and studies me, eyes moving up and down, noting the empty latte glass the waitress is removing. 'You've lost weight,' she says in an almost accusatory tone. She had always hated it if I lost weight. As I've said before, Alison's friendship is based on her sense of superiority; in her eyes I'll never be thinner, more successful or more affluent than she is, so I'm no threat.

'So what are you doing swanning around Abingdon mid-week?' She grins, showing perfectly even, laser-whitened teeth.

'Dentist appointment,' I murmur, knowing the time has finally come to do what I should have done a long time ago. 'And I was buying Joanna's birthday present.' That brings up the subject of the birthday, the whole reason I'm here.

'Ah yes, the famous birthday party. Kristen's been pestering me about her outfit, she wants a pair of Uggs.

143

I've told the childminder to take her shopping. Honestly they're so fashion-conscious now at that age. What should I get for Joanna? Could you make life easy for me and give me some pointers?'

'We'll . . . er . . . actually that's what I wanted to talk to you about, Alison.' I sit up straight and take a deep breath. I think about the look on Joanna's face when she said to me, 'Mom, I really don't want to invite Kristen to my birthday this year. She always ruins things and starts fights with Lisa. She's very mean to Lisa.'

I love Lisa Delaney, Joanna's best friend. Wide-eyed, breathless, full of enthusiasm, there isn't a malicious bone in her body and Kristen is supremely jealous of her. I remember a couple of weeks ago, Alison had asked me would I pick Kristen up from school as the childminder was sick. I'm regularly asked to pick Kristen up from school and Alison takes it for granted that I'll do it.

I listened to the three of them in the back of the car discussing Britney Spears. 'She has implants, you know. Not as big as Jordan's though. I saw it in one of my childminder's magazines,' Kristen declared.

She's so precocious, I thought, reading those sorts of magazines. Joanna and Lisa read comics.

I saw Lisa turn wide-eyed to Joanna and declare breathlessly. 'I know a celebrity that flew to America and her implants *exploded* on the plane and the heart came out with it. There was blood everywhere.'

'Oh my God!' exclaimed Joanna, agog, eyes like saucers. 'I'm *never* getting them.'

'That is *so* stupid, Lisa, You're very, very silly.' Kristen dripped contempt and sarcasm.

'That's not true, sure it's not Claire?' She tried to get me on side.

I ignored the question. 'Kristen it's rude to call someone silly. Apologize to Lisa please.'

'But—'

'Apologize please.'

'Sorry,' she muttered. 'But she *is* silly,' she said under her breath.

'Mom, I really, really don't want Kristen at my birthday 'cos she fights with my friends and please, Mom, I know that you always tell me to be kind to her but she's not a very kind girl and I just don't like her any more.'

Out of the mouths of babes. I knew exactly what my daughter meant as I sat looking at Alison. Alison and Kristen were users, pure and simple. What is the point of holding on to the friendship when neither of us has anything in common and when Alison clearly looks down her nose at me just as Kristen does with Joanna?

Why should I allow my daughter's birthday to be ruined by forcing a relationship that is not good for her? Why do I let Alison walk all over me and treat me with such disrespect? She has never appreciated any of the 'kindness' shown to her. Even my mother has gone off her. 'Got above herself, the little madam,' she said to me after we met Alison in town with a client and she barely said hello to us.

My voice is surprisingly firm as I say calmly, 'Actually, Alison, Joanna's birthday party is one of the things I want to have a little chat with you about.'

'Oh yes, planning something special? I'm going to have a marquee with a selection of entertainers for Kristen's next one,' Alison boasts as the waitress places our hot drinks in front of us.

'Nope, Joanna just wants to go to the pictures and come home and order pizza and "hang out with the gang" as she says herself,' I explain.

'Oh, lucky you! Kristen wouldn't put up with that.'

'I know, she'd think it was boring,' I agree. 'That's what I want to talk to you about. You must have noticed that for the past year and more they haven't been getting on very well.'

Alison looks startled. 'Er . . . no . . . they squabble, but all kids do that.'

'It's more than that, Alison.' I didn't want to say bluntly that Kristen is a spiteful little bitch. I couldn't be that hurtful.

'What do you mean?' She straightens up in her chair, brows drawn together, trying to frown but unable to because of the botox.

'They have nothing in common any more. You hit the nail on the head when you said that Kirsten would find the kind of party Joanna's having boring and yet, Joanna, Lisa and her friends are looking forward to "hanging out and eating pizza" immensely.'

'Oh it's just that the parties she's invited to are always catered and there's always some sort of entertainment provided, it's what the parents in our circle do. It's a pain in the ass actually, trying to come up with even bigger and better parties.' Alison throws her eyes up to heaven and I realize that success and affluence bring their own problems. Still, that's not my worry. I plough on.

'Well that's what I'm saying, Alison. Kristen moves in different circles and has higher expectations. She can be quite dismissive of Joanna and her friends and it leads to a lot of arguments,' I point out.

'Oh for God's sake, Claire, cop on, you can't let childish bickering become a big issue,' Alison snaps, beginning to see where the conversation is headed.

'It's a lot more than childish bickering, Alison,' I say, eyeballing her, annoyed by her dismissive attitude. 'And it's constant. For example, when a child tells another child that their "family time" is stupid, that's dismissive, rude and superior. When a child constantly tells a child that her best friend is a "silly twit", that's undermining, nasty behaviour. When a child taunts another child by saying that her mother earns "peanuts" that's a lot more than childish bickering in my view,' I say quietly.

Alison blushes to the roots of her dyed blonde hair. 'Oh you know the things kids say, I'm surprised at you for listening to them,' she mutters, taking a sip of green tea.

'Kids often repeat things their parents say, Alison.' I'm not letting her get away with that one, and how mean of her to let Kristen take the blame for her spiteful remark.

'Kristen didn't come up with the peanuts remark herself. I know you think my job pales in comparison to yours. I know you think Frank and I wouldn't fit in at your dinner parties. I know you didn't even give it a thought that you were twenty-five minutes late meeting me today, but my time is as precious as yours, Alison, believe it or not.

'Now, I think it's time to do the mature thing and admit that we have very, very little in common any more. Our daughters have even less, so what's the point? What's the point of hanging on to a relationship that can't by any stretch of the imagination be called a friendship? You won't miss me and I won't miss you. Be honest.'

'Don't say that. I—' Alison protested hotly.

'What's my telephone number?' I interject.

'Oh don't be ridiculous!' she snaps, flustered.

'You don't know it because the only time you ever use it is when you need me to pick Kristen up. When was the last time you rang me for a chat?'

'I'm very busy, Claire, I don't have time to be ringing people for chats,' she scowls.

'I'm very busy too, Alison believe it or not, but I always have time for my friends. I like talking to them. I need them and I'm glad to have them.'

'Oh Miss Bloody Perfect, aren't you? You always were. You with your "perfect" family growing up, and your dozens of friends and your family time and your home cooking that I never hear the end of when Kristen comes home from your place.

"Claire makes lovely dinners, why don't you?"

"Why can't we stay in a mobile home for the whole summer?"

"Joanna has family time in her house, why don't we?"

"Why can't I be Joanna's best friend?" On and on and on . . . it does my head in,' she explodes.

'Well then, it will be as much a relief for you as it will be for me if the girls don't mix any more,' I say calmly, taking a slug of much-needed coffee.

'Just because you're jealous of me is no reason to ruin our kids' friendship,' Alison counters snootily.

'Excuse me?' I almost choke on my coffee.

'Well that's what this is all about, isn't it, if you're honest? Now that we're down to the nitty gritties it galls you that I've made it; I'm successful and wealthy. You can't deal with it, clearly, but I think it's extremely childish of you to let it affect Kristen and Joanna's relationship.'

'You think I'm jealous of you?' I repeat, not sure if I'm hearing correctly.

'Aren't you . . . even a little bit?' she challenges.

Am I? Is that what this is all about . . . jealousy? Now she's made me question my motives and myself. For a moment I'm unsure and then I recognize her usual modus operandi: challenge and undermine.

'Not even the tiniest bit, Alison. Well done on everything you've achieved. You've worked hard and you deserve it but I love what I have and I wouldn't swap it for the world. Now you must excuse me, I'm pushed for time,' I say, standing up. 'Don't rush your tea. I'll pay for it on the way out. See you around.'

Alison's jaw drops. And that's the way I leave her. I don't give her time to answer. I pay the bill at the cash desk and emerge into the street, breathing in the balmy breeze, scented with spring and the promises of long, hot days to come.

I feel light-hearted, unburdened. I've done something that will affect my daughter in the most positive way and I feel really good about that. I won't miss Alison. And that's the sad thing, I suppose. I've known her thirty-five years and I'm walking away from our relationship with not an ounce of regret. We didn't have a friendship in the true sense of the word, we were just . . . a habit.

I walk briskly towards the bakery and order an extra large chocolate buttons cake, Joanna's favourite.

'Mom this is the best birthday *ever*,' she whispers to

me a week later as she and the gang 'hang out', chomping on pizza and wedges and discussing the pros and cons of choir and singing class versus speech and drama, and the various teachers involved.

'And you know something, it's great Kristen couldn't come 'cos there's no fighting, and Lisa thought it was cool!'

'You know, Kristen's not going to be around much any more. There's not much point, you don't really get on, sure you don't?' I say to my daughter. Relief washes over her.

'Not really, Mom. Is that OK?'

'Of course it's OK.' I hug her. 'You don't have to like everyone,' I explain.

'Phew, that's a relief 'cos even though I tried to, I just couldn't like that girl any more,' Joanna exclaims.

'I know, love. You did your best and that's all that matters. So forget about everything except having fun. Let's go light the candles.'

As I watch my daughter's shining face as her sister and friends bellow 'Happy Birthday', I'm overwhelmed with love for her. She did try hard with Kristen. She has a good spirit and I'm proud of her, and a little proud of myself too. I also did my best with Alison over the years, but as I explained to my daughter you don't have to like everyone and that's true for me too.

I cut the cake of 'the best party *ever*,' and watch contented as my daughter, surrounded by friends who truly love her, hands around the plates, and I smile as she gives the one with the biggest slice to Lisa Delaney.

HOLIDAYS

Recommended best beaches

ANTIGUA
Legend has it that there is a beach here for every day of the year! The top two best beaches are Dickenson Bay, in the northwest corner of the island, and Half Moon Bay, which stretches for a white-sandy mile along the eastern coast.

BARBADOS
Home to some of the finest beaches in the Caribbean especially on their 'Gold Coast', site of some of the most upmarket hotels in the Caribbean. Some of the best include Paynes Bay, Brandon's Beach, Paradise Beach, and Brighton Beach, a of which are open to the public.

BRITISH VIRGIN ISLANDS
Cane Garden Bay – Tortola, one of the Caribbean's most spectacular stretches, with over 2 miles of white sand – there's plenty of space to lay down your towel and read another short story!

GRENADA
Grand Anse Beach, a 3km (2-mile) beach is reason enough to go to Grenada. Although the island has some 45 beaches, most with white sand, this is the fabled one, and rightly so. There's enough space and so few visitors that you'll probably find a spot just for yourself. The sugary sands of Grand Anse extend into deep waters far offshore. Most of the island's best hotels are within walking distance of this beach strip.

JAMAICA
Seven Mile Beach Negril, in the north west of the island, this beach stretches for nearly 7 miles along the sea, and is overlooked by some of the most popular resorts in the Caribbean. The beach also contains some nudist sections for those who prefer au natural!

ST MAARTEN/ST MARTIN
Take your pick, the island, divided about equally between France and the Netherlands, has 39 white-sandy beaches. Popular beaches include Dawn Beach, Mullet Bay Beach, Maho Bay Beach, and Great Bay Beach on the Dutch side.

TOBAGO
Why not head to the little island of Tobago – It doesn't get any better than a long coral beach called Pigeon Point which is on the north western coast of the island. Other beaches on Tobago include Back Bay which is on the site of an old coconut plantation.

ST LUCIA
Marigot Bay, if you are looking for a private, secluded beach, you will love this strip of black sand, which is accessible only by boat. A shallow reef makes this the perfect spot for snorkeling.

Fancy sampling the sand between your toes courtesy of us?

Win a holiday for two to St Lucia

7 nights all inclusive at the Almond Morgan Bay with Virgin Holidays.

To enter the prize draw visit **virginholidays.com/prima**,
and answer the simple question.

WIN a beautiful set of Ballet swimwear or lingeri

Ballet
JUST BE

READER COMPETITION

Ballet have been producing beautiful, superbly fitting lingerie for 60 years.
To celebrate their 60th Anniversary, Ballet are giving away 60 sets of lingerie
or swimwear. We will personally select something gorgeous from our collectio
especially for you. Simply write your bra and brief size, and choose either ling
swimsuit or bikini along with your name, address, telephone number and e-ma
on a postcard and send it to: Ballet Lingerie. Prima Competition. 32 Churchill
Way. Lomeshaye Ind. Est. Nelson. Lancashire. BB9 6RT.

WIN

a  *Divine* hamper of chocolates!

CHOCOLATE

Thanks to **Divine Chocolate** we have **10 hampers** filled
to brimming with delicious Fairtrade chocolate,
each worth £40, to give away.

Simply enter online at
www.booksattransworld.co.uk/divinehamper
Terms & conditions apply
Closing date for entries is Tuesday 30 September 2008

Divine Chocolate is the delicious Fairtrade chocolate that is
co-owned by the Ghanaian cooperative of cocoa farmers, Kuapa
Kokoo, so not only do the farmers receive a fair price but they can
share in the company's profits. Divine Chocolate is made with the
best cocoa, all natural ingredients, allowing the real chocolate
flavour to come through. It's simply heavenly. You can find
Divine Chocolate in all major supermarkets as well as Oxfam
and independent stores nationwide.

For stockists and lots more information please visit
www.divinechocolate.com

Champneys
the place to be pampered

Soothe away the stresses of modern day living with a visit to a Champneys Health Resort.

Save 20% on a two night mid week break by calling 08703 300 300 and quoting Prima

Available until 19th December 2008 at all four Champneys resorts. Limited availability. Cannot be used in conjunction with any other offer.

www.champneys.com

CHAMPNEYS

EXCLUSIVE
40% DISCOUNT
at www.rbooks.co.uk

Subscribe to the Transworld Readers' Club newsletter before 30th September and not only will you automatically be eligible for a fabulous 40% off your first book order, but we'll also keep you up to speed with regular updates on a range of great books, authors, exclusive Club discounts and reader offers.

Simply go to **www.rbooks.co.uk/readersclub** to register for the newsletter and take advantage off our **40% discount** offer. And it gets better: our offer includes **FREE** postage and packing. It really couldn't be easier.